EAGLE BOY

EAGLE BOY

Rodney Bennett

CANONGATE • KELPIES

First published 1986 by Marilyn Malin Books
in association with Andre Deutsch Ltd.
First published in Kelpies 1988
Published In Canada by Optimum Publishing
International (1984) Inc., Montreal

Copyright © 1986 Rodney Bennett

Cover illustration by Alan Herriot

Printed in Great Britain
by Cox & Wyman Ltd, Reading, Berkshire

ISBN 0 86241 176 9

*The publishers acknowledge the financial assistance
of the Scottish Arts Council in the
publication of this volume*

CANONGATE PUBLISHING LTD
17 JEFFREY STREET, EDINBURGH EH1 1DR

For Jill

Part One

Exile in the mountains

'I tell you it's all because of the woodman's son.'
   'The cripple?'
'You think he's the cause of what's happened?'
'More than that — he's cast a spell on us.'
'A *spell*?'
'What does Petr say?'
'Tell us, Petr!'
'Let Petr speak!'

These appeals were directed at a thick-set, middle-aged man sitting on a rough stool. Behind him stood his wife — a quiet, shy woman who anxiously watched her husband while he hesitated, tugging at his grizzled beard. He cast troubled eyes over the sea of faces caught in the flickering rush dips placed round the room — faces like so many pale ghosts in the thick smoky atmosphere from the open fire and the odorous breath of so many people crammed together in a small space.

The village of Bletz was a community of just over two hundred people, living in low, single-storey buildings made of wood and mud with crudely thatched roofs. Many were little more than hovels, barely adequate to keep out the harsh winter weather. Petr's dwelling was larger than most, but like the rest it contained living quarters for its human occupants and a stall for animals during winter with a storage loft above. None of the buildings had windows and the only means of heating and cooking was an open fire in the middle of the living area with a hole in the roof to let out the smoke.

It was only in the castle of Bletz — a forbidding stone fortress perched on a high outcrop of rock overlooking the river that separated it from the village — that the owner boasted windows, without glass, and fireplaces with chimneys. From the ramparts the look-outs had unbroken views across a broad flat plateau with fields and meadows and many acres of natural pine forests. On clear days it was possible to see beyond the forests to the mountains in the hazy distance. Few travellers found their way to Bletz and when they did they provoked much interest. But on that cold November night a stranger could have walked or ridden into the village unnoticed, for at that moment the people of Bletz had eyes only for Petr.

He was the miller of Bletz and, even more important, the headman of the village. He had been elected by the others who admired his wisdom and steady, thoughtful leadership. They knew they could trust him to speak honestly and fairly in any disputes and over the years he had been a great champion of their traditional rights, stubbornly resisting all attempts by their feudal master, Count Boleslav, to add to his considerable powers and riches. Now, more than ever before, they were looking to Petr for guidance.

That summer the crops had failed and for the past two months there had been very little to eat. Rumours were rife everywhere; fear of starvation was in everyone's mind. Petr himself had called the meeting to give them a chance to air their anxieties and, in the course of it, the discussions had taken a dangerous turn.

Faced with so many frightened, hungry faces peering out of shapeless bundles of clothing, Petr was only too aware of their readiness to accept a scapegoat — something or someone — to blame for their hardships.

'This is a serious accusation that you make, Hans, against the woodman's child,' he began in his slow, deep voice. He was addressing a rugged, broad-shouldered man with a shock of black hair and a large black beard who stood on the edge of the crowd with arms folded across his barrel chest. This was the blacksmith, a man of great strength and a fiery temper, and he snorted loudly at the headman's words.

'But is it true?' Petr continued, scanning the rows of people squatting on the hard-trodden earth floor. 'Is it true?' he asked

4

again, looking up at the hollow-cheeked children and young mothers in the empty hay loft. Below them, two pigs grunted uneasily in a cramped stall.

'Try to think, my friends, of the real reasons for our hardships. We're all agreed the bad harvest was because we had no rain. We all saw the river and streams dry up and the earth turn to dust. We all watched our crops shrivel and die. And to add to our suffering Count Boleslav has demanded the same rents and the same tithes as in previous years — years when the harvest was good. You all know I've been many times to the Lord begging him to reduce our dues and hand back a portion of our harvest. But he refuses. My friends, there is no devil at work here, unless—' his voice dropped to a whisper so that only those nearest to him could hear '—unless it is the Lord of Bletz himself.'

'Petr, as always your words are sweet and reasonable,' the blacksmith angrily shouted. 'But you speak of things that happened after the event. I say we had no rain because the woodman's child put a curse on us. He's an evil spirit. A child of the Devil!'

A gasp went round the room. Men nodded grimly to each other; mothers clutched their infants more tightly to their breasts; the children in the loft gazed down in wide-eyed fear. No one could read or write — not even Petr — and in their ignorance of everything except the endless battle for survival, the blacksmith's words quickly took root in their superstitious minds. From all parts of the room came observations in support of Hans.

'He's not like any other child.'

'You've only to see him. Hobbling about with that vile limp.'

'He never plays with any other children — not that I'd ever let him play with mine.'

'His mother was long past the age of child-bearing when he was born.'

'When she was in labour a great bird flew over her. It never left till the child was born. She said so herself.'

'The Devil come visiting!'

At once, the room was full of low mutterings as people began saying prayers. Petr, who had been listening to these comments with growing alarm, knew he must act quickly.

'My friends,' he called, holding up his hands for silence, 'my friends, the child *is* strange. We all know this. But it's no reason for thinking he's any more the Devil's child than any one of us. Many of you have known his parents all your lives. You know, as I do, that they're honest, God-fearing people who come to Mass every Sunday —'

'But the child never comes,' a harsh voice interrupted.

'That's right. I've never seen *him* in church,' agreed another.

'Why doesn't the child attend Mass? Tell us that, Petr.'

'Very well, I'll tell you. I've often talked to his father about it and he says the child doesn't come to church because he's afraid people will laugh at him.'

The giggles from the children were quickly stifled by the women nearby.

'That's no reason for the child to stay away from Mass,' scorned a man with a pock-marked face standing beside the blacksmith. 'My son, Jiri, has a cast in one eye but he comes every Sunday.'

'Only because you drag him there, Vislav,' a peasant in the back row laughed.

The tension in the crowd eased for a moment as everyone enjoyed the joke — everyone, that is, except the angry father who glared, red-faced, at the rest.

'Friends, it's good to laugh,' Petr said. 'But perhaps we've laughed too much at Stephan.' He looked sternly up to the loft. 'You children know what I mean. He runs away from you — from all of us — because he's afraid. We have misfortunes enough, let's not add to them by making fun of this poor child.'

'Sweet talk again!' Hans shouted, pointing an accusing finger at Petr. 'We're not talking about a normal child. We're talking about a child who can't speak — except in animal grunts. A child with magic powers.'

A buzz of agreement went through the gathering. 'Do we know that he has toes on that clubbed foot of his? Or is it a cloven hoof? I tell you, he's the Devil's child and while he stays in Bletz we'll never be free from trouble.'

The response was immediate. Everyone was shouting, struggling to their feet, shaking their fists, clamouring for the child's blood. Petr shook his head in disbelief at the madness that seemed to have overtaken even the most respectable villagers, while Hans grinned in triumph at the uproar he had created.

'Well, Petr, what are we going to do?' the blacksmith demanded when at last the noise abated.

'Come on, Petr, tell us what to do,' his pock-marked neighbour chorused.

Soon the only sound in the room was the rustling of the animals in their stall as everyone waited for the headman's answer. Petr felt as though his head would burst. He knew that his silence was making the crowd restless and that he must say something soon or be open to further ridicule. With as much confidence as he could muster, he said, 'I shall speak to the priest about it.'

'The priest!' Hans exploded with a scornful laugh. 'What good will he do? He thinks of nothing but his stomach.'

This produced roars of laughter from the crowd who were well acquainted with Father Vilem's notorious appetite for food and wine. Indeed, at that very moment he was sitting with Count Boleslav in the great hall of the castle gnawing at a mutton bone, sweating with the heat of the fire and the quantity of wine he had drunk.

'I shall demand the priest goes to see the child,' Petr continued valiantly. 'I shall see that he offers prayers —'

7

'*Prayers?*' Hans bayed. 'What good are they? No, Petr, we've done with talking. If you won't help us, then we'll see to it ourselves.' He addressed the others. 'Let's go to the woodman's dwelling tonight. We'll rid ourselves of the child, once and for all.'

Immediately there were wild shouts of agreement from every part of the room and a general stampede towards the door.

Petr leaped to his feet.

'Wait!' he cried, trying to make himself heard. '*Wait!*'

Those nearest to him hesitated.

'If you won't heed what I said before, listen to me now,' Petr shouted, stopping more people. 'Don't take the law into your own hands. You'll be punished for it.'

And with these words he finally stemmed the tide of movement to the door.

'Have you thought what will happen when Count Boleslav hears of this? I beg you, don't give him cause to send the soldiers into our village.'

This grim warning struck fear in many hearts and an awkward, sullen silence fell on the crowd.

'If you're still determined to do something about the child, then do it lawfully. Go to the Lord of Bletz. Let him decide what's to be done. Choose a small group to go to the castle early tomorrow. Hans, you brought the charge against the child, it's right for you to lead them. I want no part of it. Choose for yourself the people you want to take with you. Now, all of you, go home.'

The choice of Hans as the leader of the deputation met with general approval and, in a few moments, the crowd was shuffling, sheep-like, to the door. Furious at being out-manoeuvred, the blacksmith glared at Petr and then violently pushed his way through the stragglers filing from the room.

When at last Petr and his wife were left alone, the miller slumped exhausted on to his stool.

'Fools,' he muttered, surveying the empty room.

'They're hungry — like us,' his wife stated flatly.

'That's no reason to kill an innocent child.'

'*Is* he innocent?'

Petr stared at his wife.

'You too?'

She shrugged and wearily moved to cover the fire with clods of turf — a nightly ritual in each household to avoid the risk of fire when everyone was asleep. She heard her husband get to his feet, but it was only when the door banged that she realized he had intended to go out. She called half-heartedly after him, and sighed. She had learned many years ago that once Petr set his mind to do something, there was little she could do or say to stop him.

2

The night air struck cold on Petr's face. A watery halo circled the moon, but the stars were bright. He glanced at the dark silhouette of the castle looming above him, then set off at a brisk pace in the opposite direction along the deserted track through the village.

As he marched through the night, he went over in his mind the plan that had come to him in the closing moments of the meeting. It was a desperate plan and he shook his head at the thought of it. But if he could persuade the woodman to go through with it, the child would at least have a fighting chance of survival.

Arriving at a huge gnarled oak tree that marked the mile post from the village, Petr left the track and followed a footpath skirting ploughed fields. In the moonlight, the long dark shadows of the furrows looked deceptively tranquil. It was hard to believe they were the scene of so much back-breaking labour. For generations, the peasants had toiled in these fields for successive Lords of Bletz and Petr wondered, as he had done many times before, why one man should rule the lives of so many others; why one man should be rich and live in a castle while the rest were poor and hungry. As ever, he could find no answer to these questions and was forced to conclude that this was how things had always been and would always remain — the Lord's soldiers would see to that.

With the ploughed fields behind him, he was now crossing open meadow land, glistening with hoar-frost. Away in the distance, a low mist hung over the river — the river that in summer had been reduced to a heart-breaking trickle.

As the long, dark shape of the forest became discernible, Petr quickened his pace. For all his years and the distance he had already come, he broke into a jog-trot, heading towards the lofty shapes of three great oak trees. Behind them was

Josef the woodman's dwelling, one of several dotted about the edge of the forest housing Count Boleslav's woodmen.

Petr had known Josef all his life. They had grown up as boys together — Petr always the stockier of the two and Josef who was like a young sapling as a youth and a near giant standing over six feet by early manhood. Petr had been present when Josef was betrothed to Marta, a girl of the village. He had shared their long years of disappointment when it seemed that Marta — like his own wife — was barren; and their joy when at last she became pregnant. He had suffered with them when their son, Stephan, was born a cripple and, later, when he failed to speak.

The thought of Stephan's handicap and strangeness made him frown and, as he reached the oak trees, his resolve suddenly weakened. Steadying himself against the rough bark of one of the trees while he regained his breath, he ran his tongue over frozen lips and looked at the hut built by Josef's father.

Was he wrong? Was it possible that Stephan might be an evil child? He alone had spoken up for the boy — even his own wife had agreed with the others. He had not expected to see Josef or Marta at the meeting, for it was a long walk to the village at night. But could there be a more sinister reason for their absence? Did they know something about their son which needed to be kept secret? And yet it was unthinkable that any child of Josef and Marta could be a creature of the Devil. The anger which rose up inside him at such a monstrous idea gave him the impetus to go on. He ran the last few yards and banged on the door.

It took a while before there was any response from inside. Then he heard scuffling noises and a gruff, suspicious voice demanding, 'Who's there?'

'It's me, Petr.'

Footsteps approached the door, a wooden bolt was draw back, and the door opened to reveal a tall, grey-haired figure bent forward in the low doorway. He was dressed in a long tunic and in his hands was a large axe.

'Petr!' the woodman exclaimed, dropping the axe to his side. 'What brings you here in the middle of the night?'

'I must speak to you, old friend,' Petr whispered.

The urgency in his voice made Josef quickly beckon him inside.

'What is it? What's happening?' a woman's sleepy voice asked.

'It's only Petr,' Josef grunted. He drew a piece of glowing kindling from beneath the clods on the fire and held it to a rush dip. As the reeds dipped in mutton fat took light, they revealed a woman sitting up on a straw mattress. Seeing the visitor, Marta modestly draped herself in a coarse blanket and got out of bed.

'We were asleep —' Josef began, running a large hand through his tousled hair. Then the look on Petr's face made him stop. 'What is it?' he asked in alarm.

'It's Stephan.'

'Stephan?'

Petr quickly told them about the violent scene at the meeting. 'It's hunger that makes them say these things. I tried to persuade them otherwise, but they wouldn't listen. Some of them are going to the castle tomorrow. They'll say Stephan is a child of the Devil and demand his death.'

Josef and Marta stared at Petr in speechless horror. Then little cries like a dog whining made them turn towards a dark corner where a child was sitting and rubbing his eyes.

This was Stephan — the object of so much fear and hatred. He was a small, slight figure who looked younger than his eight years. In the flickering light of the rush dip, his pale oval face — paler than usual in his drowsy state — and shock of golden hair combined to give him a haunting quality of innocence. Through bewildered eyes — dark pinpoints in the half light — he looked up at the three adults. Sitting like this in a loose tunic with his legs hidden beneath the blankets, he gave no hint of being a cripple.

Marta gave a heart-rending cry and threw herself down beside her son.

'They won't hurt you,' she sobbed, holding him tightly. 'I'll see they don't hurt you.'

'Grr. . . Gr . . . ,' the child grunted, looking anxiously from one face to the next.

'There's not a moment to lose,' Petr whispered to Josef. 'You must take him into hiding at once.'

The woodman, who was a man of few words, slowly nodded.

'We'll all go,' he said. 'To the forest.'

'No, that's not the way. If you all go, they'll know you've gone into hiding and the soldiers will come looking for you.'

'What then?'

Petr hesitated. Now that the moment had come to explain his plan, his heart quailed at the distress he would be inflicting on his friends.

'Listen to me carefully,' he said, taking a deep breath. 'There is only one way to stop the soldiers looking for Stephan. You must say he was taken away by the Devil.'

'You mean, *agree* with them?' Marta cried. 'Never. *Never.*'

'Hush woman,' her husband remonstrated, trying to take in what the headman had just told them. He turned anxiously to his old friend. 'You're not telling us to hide Stephan by himself, are you?'

'Believe me, I don't say this lightly. It's the only way.'

'You mean, live by himself in the forest?'

'No. Not the forest.'

'Then where?'

Petr looked at the floor, unable to bring himself to speak.

'Where? Where then?'

'In the mountains,' Petr said in a low, gruff voice.

For a moment, the woodman stared at him in total disbelief.

Then, realizing that Petr was in earnest, he began to shake with anger.

'The *mountains*!' he raged. 'It'd kill the boy.'

'Not necessarily.' Petr was speaking more freely now with his eyes fixed on Josef. 'Stephan is young and strong. There are caves in the mountains. You can take him food — secretly. And no one will think of looking for him there.'

He paused, waiting for a response from the woodman. But the poor man could only shake his head. Desperately, Petr appealed to Marta.

'It may only be for one night,' he said. 'Who knows what the Lord will say tomorrow. But if it has to be longer, a good harvest next year will put everything right. People will have forgotten and you can bring Stephan home. Please, I beg you. There's so little time. We must get him to safety.'

Marta's tear-stained face looked at Petr in an agony of indecision. Then, in a voice that was barely more than a whisper, she said, 'I'll get him dressed.'

But there was a wild bellow from the woodman who seized his axe, rushed to the door and threw it wide open.

'Come, all of you,' he roared into the night. 'I'll kill you all before you lay a hand on my son.'

Petr came up behind him and laid a hand on his shoulder.

'Save your energies for the journey,' he said gravely, and all the rage left Josef. The axe dropped to his side and his shoulders sagged.

'Get yourself dressed,' Petr said, gently trying to prod him into action. 'And cover up well. It'll be very cold in the mountains.'

The woodman nodded silently. In slow, resigned movements, he closed the door, leant the axe against a wall and moved into the room to gather up his clothes.

Marta had almost finished dressing Stephan and was on her knees binding the child's feet with straw and sacking. Petr winced at the sight of the ugly clubbed foot and the way

Marta's fingers moved clumsily in her agitation, making the boy upset and herself more flustered.

'That's good,' the headman said to give encouragement. 'He'll need all the warm things you can find.'

The small dark room was now a flurry of movement as Marta ran about looking for odd pieces of sacking and sheepskins to tie over Stephan's shoulders. And, for the first time, it was possible to see the extent of Stephan's handicap. Still drugged with sleep and bewildered by the strange happenings, he limped awkwardly after his mother. But the over-sized bundle on his right foot dragged heavily on the floor and he began to make anxious whimpering sounds. He tried to clutch at Marta's shift as she hurried past and almost pushed her over.

'Get out of my way,' she cried. 'Can't you see I'm busy?'

The child burst into tears and hobbled away to the dark corner of the room where only a short time ago he had been sleeping peacefully. Confused and frightened, he continued to cry until his father, swathed in sheepskins, gathered him up in his arms.

The sight of the child hobbling about the room and now weeping in his father's arms filled Petr with dismay. He could not imagine how the boy would ever make the journey to the mountains.

'I'll carry him,' the woodman said, sensing what was going through his mind.

'It's a long way.'

'I'll manage.'

Marta hurried forward with a bundle of provisions, saying, 'There's bread, apples, cheese, nuts — enough for a week.' She spoke bravely as she tied the bundle round Josef's shoulders but, once it was done, she turned away to hide her tears.

The two old friends faced each other grimly.

'Be gone,' Petr said, clasping father and son in a brief bear-like hug.

Josef nodded and turned to Marta. For a moment, they saw their own anguish reflected in each other's eyes. There was so much to say, but no time to say it, and no words to express how they felt.

Quickly Marta stepped forward, threw another shawl around Stephan's shoulders and lightly kissed him on the cheek.

'God have mercy on us,' she whispered.

'Amen,' the two men replied.

'Be careful, husband,' she said, giving him a tremulous kiss.

Josef managed a smile and turned to the door which Petr was holding open for him.

'Don't linger,' the headman said. 'Remember you must be at work when the soldiers arrive.'

With the briefest of acknowledgements, the woodman stepped out into the night and, with the child falling asleep in his arms, hurried away.

Petr stood watching them disappear into the darkness under the trees. He could hear Marta sobbing in the room behind him and he could not help feeling worried about the wisdom of his plan.

Stephan's journey into exile had begun.

3

A dank, cold mist lingered in the courtyard of the castle as two bleary-eyed soldiers emerged from the gatehouse and marched to the main gate. They banged their leather gloves together to get warm, making sharp reports that echoed round the high stone walls like the wings of a large river bird beating the surface of the water. Pulling together, the men drew back three heavy iron bolts and in turn heaved open two massive wooden doors studded with iron nails. Outside, swathed in sheepskins and sacking, the deputation of four peasants was already waiting for them.

'We've come to speak to the Lord of Bletz,' Hans said, swaggering forward.

The younger of the two guards laughed. 'At this hour!'

'What d'you want with him?' the other growled.

'Private matters — for the Lord's ears only.'

'It's urgent,' said Vislav, the pock-marked peasant who had spoken up for his squint-eyed son, Jiri.

'The Lord will bless us for our troubles,' a third peasant sniffed. He was Lobvic, the carpenter of Bletz — a lanky, beardless man of fanatical religious views.

'No one enters unless he states his business.'

'We've already told you —' Vislav began.

'It's the *law*,' the soldier snapped.

'The Lord won't be pleased when he learns we came with news about sorcery,' Hans retorted, turning on his heel with a pretence of leaving.

'Wait!'

Hans winked at the others and ambled back to the guards.

'Sorcery you say?' the older guard asked warily. His companion rubbed the stubble on his chin with the back of a glove.

The blacksmith nodded.

The guard hesitated, then said, 'You'd better enter.'

Grinning broadly, Hans led the deputation into the courtyard.

'Wait here,' the older guard ordered. A jerk of his head sent the other soldier back to the gate while he marched off to the guardhouse.

The deputation congratulated Hans on his skilful handling of the soldiers. Only the youngest of the peasants, Matthias, showed any sign of nervousness.

'D'you really think the Lord will be pleased?' he asked timidly.

'Course he will,' Vislav snorted.

'We discussed it all last night,' Hans growled. 'There's no turning back now.'

At that moment a wooden cart laden with barrels and sacks of vegetables entered through the gateway. It was drawn by a lumbering ox that puffed and blew hot breath from the effort of pulling a heavy load up the steep track to the castle. It passed close by the deputation, making them leap out of the way of the mud thrown up by the wheels.

'Never forget, Matthias,' Hans scowled as they regrouped, '*that's* what it's all about — food.'

'The whole village is behind us,' Vislav added, looking in disgust at the filth on his leggings fresh on that morning.

Matthias flushed a bright red and bowed his head.

For nearly an hour they hung about, waiting to hear whether they would be seen by Count Boleslav. From time to time soldiers in conical helmets and chain mail over leather jerkins emerged from the guardhouse to take up their stations and set about their duties. At one point, a troop of horses already saddled were led from the stables by young grooms to a group of waiting cavalry men. Once mounted, they clattered off across the cobbles, laughing and shouting to the soldiers on the gates.

Then, above the general noise and bustle, came the sound of a horn announcing that the Lord of Bletz had risen.

'Don't forget to kneel,' Hans reminded the others.

'And speak loudly,' Vislav added, sounding like the second-in-command he was.

'Christ is on our side,' Vislav said with a superior smile.

'Supposing the Lord doesn't agree with us. What happens then?' Matthias asked.

'You're worse than a frightened old woman,' the blacksmith growled. He was beginning to regret the inclusion of Matthias, who had been chosen because of his popularity with the other villagers, having a good voice for leading the singing in the fields.

'What's your business, peasants?'

The unexpectedness and sternness of the voice making this demand startled them. With one accord they turned to find themselves confronted by a tall, muscular soldier whose appearance and manner indicated a man of authority. A long green and yellow cloak hung over his armour and his sword was already drawn. Behind him stood two pikemen and the guard they had met at the gate.

'We've come to speak to the Lord of Bletz,' Hans boldly replied.

The soldier, who was no less than the assistant commander of the garrison, regarded the blacksmith with lofty suspicion.

'Your name?'

'Hans. The blacksmith.'

The soldier received the news without comment and turned to the others.

'Vislav from the Long Acre.'

'Lobvic —'

'Ah yes,' the soldier interjected, showing interest for the first time, 'the priest has spoken of you.'

Lobvic's pasty face flushed with pleasure.

'I made the new benches for the church — '

'He says you're a trouble-maker.'

The thin carpenter was instantly reduced to jelly and automatically scratched his long nose — a nervous habit whenever he was upset or embarrassed.

Meanwhile, the assistant commander waited for the last member of the deputation to introduce himself.

'Ma . . . Ma . . . Mat-thias,' he stuttered. 'From the M . . . M . . . Middle Field.'

The soldier sniffed and returned to Hans.

'I'm told you have news of sorcery.'

'We do.'

'Who do you charge?'

'That's for the Lord's ears.'

The soldier bristled with rage. There was a flash of steel and his sword was at Hans' throat. Then, changing his mind, he gave a mirthless chuckle and dropped the sword to his side.

'Your accusation had better be correct, blacksmith,' he warned. 'Take them inside,' he snapped to the two pikemen. 'Soldier —' this was directed at the guard they had first met '— back to your station.'

With the assistant commander leading the way, the deputation was escorted across the courtyard to the keep and through an arched doorway into the great hall of the castle where even Hans wilted a little at the impressive sight which greeted them.

The great hall was a high-ceilinged chamber with massive timbers supporting the roof. Tapestries depicting hunting scenes hung on the walls and, in the sombre morning light coming through a row of narrow arched windows high up near the roof, the coloured threads contrasted richly with the grey stone walls.

At each end of a long oak table set across the chamber, two small groups of men dressed for hunting in bright hats and fur-trimmed robes stood watching the entry of the peasants with faint amusement. Behind the table, at its centre, sat a slight, sardonic man whose narrow face was framed with a well-trimmed beard and long dark hair showing beneath a conical hat edged with sable fur. Over his red and yellow tunic he wore a long over-robe entirely made of sable.

The Lord of Bletz, Count Boleslav, watched with languid indifference as the peasants fell on their knees, foreheads almost touching the floor. His fingers lightly played with a miniature hunting horn made of solid silver hanging from an amber necklace. Behind him, in breastplate and armour on arms and legs, stood the formidable figure of the commander of the garrison, a bull-necked man with closely cropped hair and a deep scar running across the coarse skin on his face.

The assistant commander stepped forward and saluted.

'These are the peasants, my Lord. They say they will only speak to you.'

'Then let them speak.' Count Boleslav's voice was light but without a trace of warmth. The men at each end of the table gave a polite, well-practised titter.

Hans raised his head and in a rough, hoarse voice embarked on his prepared speech.

'My Lord, we've come asking for a judgement. Our headman told us to do this —'

'Where is the miller?' Count Boleslav interjected. 'Why isn't he here?'

'He refused to come, my Lord.'

'Oh? Why?'

'My Lord, I don't know,' the blacksmith lied.

Count Boleslav made no further comment, but sniffed a small embroidered silk bag stuffed with cloves. He had planned to spend the morning hunting wild boar in the forest and was eager to be rid of the peasants who were filling the chamber with foul odours.

'My Lord,' Hans continued, trying to pick up the threads of his speech, 'we're suffering many hardships. Our barns are empty, and we are hungry . . .'

21

The onlookers stared in disbelief at the peasant who seemed oblivious of the danger in what he was saying. Count Boleslav was now very still and was studying the blacksmith through hooded eyes.

'. . . We've discussed the cause of our troubles,' Hans was saying, 'and we're all agreed we have an evil spirit in Bletz.'

The unexpectedness of this made the lordly gathering gasp — even Count Boleslav looked surprised.

'What evil spirit is this?' he asked sharply.

'My Lord, a child. The son of one of your Lordship's woodmen.'

'A vile cripple, my Lord,' Vislav added.

'What is the child's name?'

'Stephan, my Lord. The son of Josef.'

Count Boleslav received this information in silence. He settled back into his chair, sniffing the bag of cloves, while his entourage waited expectantly, trying to assess the reaction of the cool, impassive face.

'What evidence do you have?' Count Boleslav finally asked.

'We've suspected it for a long time,' Hans said grandly. 'If you saw him you would know at once that he's no ordinary child.'

'He talks in animal grunts,' Vislav said.

'And never comes to Mass,' Lobvic added. 'He's ungodly.'

'His own father admits this,' the blacksmith declared. 'It's that clubbed foot of his. People say it's a cloven hoof.'

'He's c . . . cast a spell on our crops,' Matthias stammered.

'It's an evil child, my Lord,' Hans boomed, 'and we ask for it to be destroyed.'

Several minutes passed before Count Boleslav spoke. He was unmoved by the peasants' hardships but, at the same time, he was well aware of them. Indeed, he had already instructed the commander of the garrison to deal firmly with any disturbances that might occur in the village. The peasants seemed to be offering a convenient explanation for their deprivations but, like everyone else, sorcery made him uneasy. Under the circumstances, he decided to seek expert advice.

'Well, priest, what have you to say about this?'

He was addressing the fat man in a greasy black habit who was sitting a little way down the table.

For all his gross appearance and the quantities of food and wine that he consumed, Father Vilem's mind was surprisingly agile. It needed to be for the continuation of all the advantages he enjoyed. Many years ago he had decided that his immediate well-being depended more on his earthly ruler than his heavenly one and he worked hard at keeping Count Boleslav happy.

Now he was being asked his opinion on the tricky question of witchcraft and he thought carefully before giving a reply.

'My Lord, I've suspected this child for some time,' he lied with practised ease. 'I've often prayed for him. But we cannot save those who are not ours to save. The Devil, unlike our Saviour, does not like to go unnoticed and the clubbed foot is undoubtedly an outward sign of the child's unholy nature. My advice, therefore, is trial by fire. If the child survives, he will be cleansed of all impurities. If not, then Bletz will be well rid of a malevolent spirit.'

After a speech like this, there was only one course of action.

'Send a troop to seize the child,' Count Boleslav said airily. 'But I should like to see this clubbed foot before it is put to the fire.'

The commander saluted and, with a nod, dispatched his assistant to give the necessary orders. Count Boleslav dismissed the peasants with a perfunctory wave and got up to go.

'My Lord,' the fat priest whispered. 'Would it not be politic to reward them for their services?'

The Lord of Bletz looked sharply at him, then smiled.

'It is a good shepherd,' he said, 'who knows his flock. Give each man a half measure of grain. And blacksmith, tell the miller I require to know the reason for his absence.'

'My Lord, I will,' Hans replied with relish.

Amid shouts from the deputation and polite applause from the assembly, the Lord of Bletz swept from the chamber, keenly anticipating a whole day given over to sport.

4

Stumbling through the forest, gasping for breath, Josef's eyes kept returning to the faint patch of lightness above the trees. It was here that the sun was hidden behind the clouds and it meant that the morning was already well advanced. He feared that by the time he reached home the soldiers would have already come and gone.

When at last his dwelling came into view he stopped for a moment, holding on to a tree, while he searched for evidence of visitors. Everything looked peaceful. The pile of logs he had been chopping the day before stood undisturbed. The dwelling itself seemed quiet with a familiar trail of smoke rising from the roof. Perhaps, after all, the soldiers had not yet arrived. Summoning some last reserves of strength, he ran to the hut and fell against the door. As Marta opened it he collapsed into her arms.

'Have they come?' he managed to gasp. And to his great relief she shook her head.

Marta helped him inside to the fire where he slumped on to a stool while she removed his wet outer garments. Then she hurried away to fill a wooden bowl with the broth she had kept simmering in a pot hanging over the fire. Kneeling in front of him, she urged him to take sips from a spoon which she held out for him. Between mouthfuls he began to tell her about the cave where he had left Stephan.

He had almost come to the end of his story when faint sounds in the distance filled them with dread. The pounding of approaching hooves could mean only one thing. There was no time for more words. Josef struggled to his feet, quickly embraced Marta, who had turned white, seized his axe and ran outside.

By the time the troop of six horsemen came galloping round the oak trees, Josef looked as though he had been chopping logs since sunrise. They surrounded him in a tight ring, close enough for him to feel the horses' steaming breath and sweating flanks. He looked up with feigned surprise, all sign of fatigue gone but alert and tense inside.

'We've come for the child,' the captain of the troop barked.

Josef fell to his knees, assuming a woeful expression.

'Oh sir, he's not here.'

'What d'you mean, peasant?'

'He was taken from us last night.'

The captain snorted and drew his sword to beat the woodman with the flat of the blade. Josef flinched but continued.

'He was playing out here as usual, when —' he paused to look round at Marta who was standing in the doorway. Then, in a loud voice so that she could hear, he said, 'When a creature flew out of the sky and carried him off.'

The words had come tumbling out of him and he bowed his head, conscious of the ring of stony faces staring at him.

'Fetch the woman,' the captain snapped without taking his eyes from Josef.

Two soldiers dismounted and dragged Marta into the circle, throwing her on the ground beside her husband.

'Is this true, woman?'

'Every word, sir,' Marta said in a frightened voice. 'A huge black creature it was, with giant wings and a long tail. It landed just where you are now, sir.'

Instinctively, the soldiers reigned in their mounts, glancing uneasily about them. Silently, Josef applauded Marta's invention.

'Search the place,' the captain barked.

The banging and clattering which followed indicated that the soldiers who had gone into the dwelling were turning the place upside-down. A few moments later, they emerged shaking their heads.

The captain frowned. He had been prepared for resistance — was even looking forward to it — but he had not bargained for this. He would have to return to the castle — but not empty-handed.

'Tie them up,' he ordered.

Josef gave Marta a reassuring smile as thick ropes were tied round their shoulders, pinning their arms to their sides. Then the soldiers remounted and, on the command of the captain, they spurred the horses forward, jerking the helpless couple to their feet.

Hauled along at the end of the ropes, the woodman and his wife were forced to run, stumbling and lurching, to keep pace with the relentless trotting hooves. They crossed the meadows and the fields where peasants looked up from their labours and wondered why Josef and Marta were being taken to the castle and not their son. In the village, people too old or sick to work appeared at doorways and, with frightened, sullen faces, watched the couple's progress. Someone ran to tell the blacksmith; another, kinder spirit, went in search of the miller. Ignoring the bridge, the soldiers rode their horses through a shallow crossing in the river, drenching their captives who arrived at the other side like drowned rats. Unable to run any more, they could only submit to being dragged up the rutted track to the castle and across the cobbled courtyard where the crowd scattered before the horsemen. The captain held up his hand and, mercifully, the trotting hooves came to a stop.

Soaked to the skin, bruised and cut, Josef and Marta lay huddled together, while the crowd gathered round to peer at the grey-haired giant and the weeping woman bound with ropes. Josef and Marta were too exhausted and too full of pain to notice what was going on around them until rough hands seized the ropes and, once more, they were jerked to their feet.

In the great hall, the Lord of Bletz stood fuming with his back to a blazing fire. Two hounds barked at him, urging him to continue with the game which had been interrupted by the arrival of the captain. Until then, Count Boleslav had been in a particularly jocular mood — the boar hunt had been a great success and he had been throwing bones around the chamber for the dogs to chase after. While the two powerful animals raced about, leaping on the long table and even running along it, the other huntsmen laid bets on which hound would reach a bone first.

As Josef and Marta were dragged into the chamber, Count Boleslav aimed a vicious kick at the dogs.

'Take them away,' he ordered, and two luckless servants, braving the snapping teeth, ran to obey.

The bedraggled, trembling couple fell to their knees in front of the Lord of Bletz and he looked at them through cold, dark eyes.

'Where is the child?' His voice was like sharpened steel.

At first, they were both speechless with fear. But then the low tittering in the crowd made Josef angry and he found his voice.

'My Lord, our son was taken from us last night,' he said. 'A huge flying creature came out of the sky and carried him off.'

Count Boleslav received this news in silence and, for a moment, stared at Josef as though trying to read the mind behind the scratched, dirty face. Then, abruptly, he snapped, 'Fetch the priest.'

While a servant hurried away, the Lord of Bletz strolled to the long table with his sable robe sweeping the floor behind him. A mood of hushed expectation descended on the chamber as he sat on a high-backed chair, lightly drumming the table with slender fingers.

For several minutes no one moved, or spoke. Then the silence was broken by sounds of a commotion outside and, in a few moments, the blacksmith was hustled in.

'So!' Count Boleslav remarked stonily. 'It seems you sent my soldiers on a wild goose chase, blacksmith.' His eyes went to the door as Petr, covered in flour, was escorted in. 'And the

28

miller too.' His voice was loaded with sarcasm. 'We are indeed privileged to have *your* presence.'

Petr knelt on one knee, head bowed.

'My Lord,' he said, 'I have come to plead for this man and woman.'

'And what about their son?'

'My Lord, the peasants who came this morning came with my full knowledge. But not with my support.'

'Be careful what you say, miller. The child has already been found guilty.'

'Then my Lord,' Petr said in his deep, steady voice, 'I beg that you'll show mercy to his parents. They are honest, loyal peasants who would do nothing wrong.'

'They've hidden the child — that's what they've done,' Hans shouted, pointing accusingly at Josef and Marta.

'Enough!' Count Boleslav snapped. 'I wish to hear no more from you, blacksmith.'

Hans hung his head, glaring at the floor.

At that moment, a door at the back of the chamber opened and in waddled the fat priest, puffing and blowing.

'Well!' Count Boleslav smiled. 'It seems I have need of you for a second time in one day.'

Father Vilem bowed.

'My Lord, as God's servant and yours,' he panted, 'I wish it were a hundred times a day.'

'Then let's see if your wisdom matches your flattery,' Count Boleslav said with only the ghost of a smile.

Father Vilem gave another bow and concentrated on hiding the apprehension he felt at the sight of the kneeling peasants. Something had clearly gone wrong with the seizure of the child.

'Woodman, tell the priest your story,' Count Boleslav commanded.

Josef looked guiltily at Father Vilem, worried at having to lie before a priest, even one of ill-repute. But, having no

29

alternative, he said, 'Our son, Stephan, was taken from us last night by a creature that flew out of the sky. It was a huge, black thing, Father, with great wings and a long tail. It picked the boy up and carried him off. We've not seen him since.'

'Why didn't you come to me?' the priest asked, playing for time. He was feeling rather sick after running to the chamber and because of the awkward situation that he was now in.

'Oh Father, we were afraid to,' Marta sobbed, coming to the aid of her husband.

Petr was delighted with the tale his friends had devised, but wondered whether it was plausible enough to satisfy the devious minds of the Lord and his priest.

'So, this is the conundrum,' Count Boleslav was saying in a light, but deadly voice that made the fat priest feel even more nauseated. 'Do we believe the story — or not? Do we hang these two and go on searching for the child? Or do we say, this is the Devil's work?'

Father Vilem mopped the sweat from his brow and tried to think. He knew there was no way of telling if the story were true or false. If he declared it to be false, then Count Boleslav would order the execution of the parents and dispatch soldiers to look for the child — a great deal of trouble which, if it proved fruitless, might rebound on him. If, on the other hand, he declared it to be true, it would at least agree with his previous judgement and, perhaps, impress Count Boleslav with his knowledge. Father Vilem began to feel a little better.

'My Lord, this affair need hardly trouble you at all,' he began. 'I have read many books describing the various manifestations of the Devil.' This was quite untrue, but was calculated to impress his authority on a gathering in which he was one of the very few who could read at all. 'The creature which these peasants claim to have seen is indeed a common form — the large wings, the long tail, and so on. Perhaps, having some evil knowledge of the child's capture, the Devil assumed this bird-like guise to remove his creature to safety.'

Count Boleslav frowned.

'What are you saying, priest? Are you telling me the story is true?'

'Indeed, my Lord. That's exactly what I'm saying.' Father Vilem was now speaking quite affably. He was well pleased with his speech and the queasiness in his stomach had almost gone.

'What about the Devil's child? Do we search the forest?'

'That, of course, is in your hands, my Lord. But my opinion is that this creature has been taken much further away.'

Josef and Marta, who had found it difficult to understand the priest's speech, could hardly believe their ears, for it seemed Father Vilem had fallen for their story. Josef had to bite his lips to stop himself laughing out loud. Beside him, Marta felt faint with relief. She bowed her head, not from shame or fear, but to hide her tears of joy.

'And what shall we do with these two?' they heard Count Boleslav ask, making them afraid once more.

Having scored such a success with his display of learning, Father Vilem thought it appropriate now to display Christian charity, tempered with discipline.

'These are simple creatures, my Lord, with not enough wit to pray for their own souls. Rather than hang them, why not let me make an example of them? I'll see they make penance for the trouble they have given you. They will be made to attend Mass on three successive Sundays, bare-headed and bare-footed, and dressed in sackcloth.'

'So be it,' the Lord of Bletz decreed. He had suddenly become bored with the whole affair. Having been denied the spectacle of the child being put to the fire, the hanging of two wretched peasants offered little amusement. He stood up to leave when there was an outburst from the blacksmith.

'My Lord, these two have reared an evil spirit. Surely they should be punished more than that?'

Petr was immediately on his feet.

'My Lord, as headman of Bletz, I swear that no charge has ever been made against this couple. They are well liked and no one wishes them harm.'

'Silence!' The order came from the commander of the garrison and his voice made everyone freeze.

'Blacksmith, be warned,' Count Boleslav said with deadly menace. 'Last time you left this chamber with a reward. Be thankful you leave now without punishment.' His eyes flicked to the commander who dispatched two soldiers with a jerk of his head to seize Hans and quickly remove him from the chamber.

Without another word, the Lord of Bletz strode out to the accompaniment of polite clapping from the other huntsmen. Following quickly behind his master, the fat priest contrived to take some of this applause for himself.

While soldiers untied the ropes, Josef and Marta smiled unashamedly at each other, and at Petr. Free to go, they slowly walked from the chamber.

Hans was waiting for them as they came out. He spat on the ground at their feet. 'Don't think you've won,' he growled, and stalked away.

'Take no notice of him,' Petr said evenly. 'Tell me, did you get Stephan to safety?' he asked in a low voice.

Josef nodded.

'Good. That's all I need to know. Now we must part. We mustn't be seen talking together.'

The journey home took the woodman and his wife a long time. They were very tired and their injuries throbbed and ached. Josef held Marta's arm and each step seemed to require great effort.

It was raining by the time they reached their dwelling and, as they entered, it felt damp and smelt of stale broth.

Furniture and belongings were strewn about and the fire had gone out. But at least they could look at each other without fear.

5

Stephan was roused from sleep by a gentle pressure nudging his right cheek. It made his face twitch and, with eyes still half-closed, his hand went lazily to his cheek touching a soft furry body that darted away with a small cry. He opened his eyes and found himself looking at a white hare. It was flattened to the ground, ears back, poised for flight.

In his drowsy state, Stephan thought he must have fallen asleep in the forest but, as his eyes focused on the rocky ceiling and walls, he immediately stiffened and sat bolt upright. The hare scampered away, whimpering piteously from an injury on its back. Now, wide awake, Stephan looked again at his surroundings, frowning at their strangeness.

He called out, but there was no reply. Mystified and anxious, he got up and limped outside. A cool, stiff breeze blew his hair over his face and as he tried to hold it from his eyes with one hand, the other reached for a rock to steady himself, for the sight which greeted him came like a blow to the head.

He could not understand what had happened. All the familiar sights of home were gone — the grassy patch where he had played since infancy, the oak trees and the pine forest — and in their place were bare, jagged rocks and long sweeping slopes covered with freshly fallen snow. Nervously, he edged forward to find himself looking down a dizzy cataract of water plunging into a dark pool a hundred feet below.

Twisting round, he was confronted by high, precipitous cliffs that soared upwards until they were swallowed up in the clouds. The dark, towering masses of rock swam dangerously before his eyes and he almost lost his balance.

In strange, unformed words he began to shout for his mother and father. But all he could hear in reply was the thunder of the waterfall. Panic-stricken, he stumbled back to the cave where he fell in a heap, clasping a blanket to his mouth, unable to understand why he was not at home, surrounded by the familiar smells of bodies mixed with straw and smoke and cooking. His face crumpled, and he began to cry.

As he sat with knees up to his chest, sucking the blanket, memories of what he thought must be a dream kept returning to him. A strange man came to his home in the middle of the night. His mother's face was pale and angry. Her unplaited hair hung down to her shoulders and she kept running away. His father carried him through a snow storm. He could hear his father's voice but the face was always hidden in darkness. Above all, these fragments were associated with an overwhelming feeling of danger and he tried to blot them out by burrowing in to the blankets.

Throughout that first day in exile, Stephan repeatedly went outside, shouting, imploring his parents to come. But they never answered and, as darkness fell, he lay wrapped in the blankets in a tight little ball, crying and shivering, until sleep finally overtook him. The bundle of food lay untouched on the floor.

Next morning, he was on his feet as soon as he was awake, limping outside and yelling with all the strength in his small body. He stood for a long time, straining for the sound of a reassuring voice above the roar of the water and the howling wind. Very frightened and lonely, he slumped down on a rock where he remained for most of the day.

In the late afternoon, a sudden fall of snow forced him to seek refuge in the cave. Exhaustion and weakness from lack of food overtook him and, mercifully, he fell asleep.

Dawn on the third day found him already outside yelling with tears streaming down his face. He was like a frightened animal blindly calling for help, no longer aware of what he was doing — or why. And it was a purely animal instinct which later drove him inside, not to seek comfort in his blankets, but in the darkest regions at the rear of the cave. Crouched in a narrow space, too terrified to move, he became oblivious of the passing daylight hours and the hours of darkness which followed.

In those slow, stagnant hours, he withdrew into a trance-like state — not asleep or unconscious, but suspended in a limbo where time and place ceased to exist. Like a pond drying up in the hot sun, all knowledge of his previous life, all memories of people, things and places, were gradually drained out of him. He was left an empty shell, waiting for the moment when he could begin a new life.

It began soon after daybreak on the fourth day with small convulsions in his arms and fingers. Soon these involuntary spasms spread until his whole body trembled. After reaching a climax they slowly faded and, when his body was still, he took a deep breath and exhaled it in a sigh.

Like someone discovering the use of their limbs for the first time, he stood upright and stretched his arms above his head, letting them drop in two opposing arcs to his side. Then, with head held inquisitively on one side, he slowly limped towards the light. He stopped for a moment, frowning in surprise at the dragging weight of his right foot, and hobbled forward again with a hand on a wall of the cave to steady himself, alert but relaxed, like an animal exploring new territory.

The sight of the hare sniffing the bundle of provisions made him pause. The animal looked up in alarm and, as he moved closer, it hopped away to a safe distance. Stephan knelt beside the mysterious parcel and sniffed it. The smells suddenly made him feel ravenously hungry and he grabbed the bundle, shaking it until a knot gave way, scattering the contents on the floor. At once, the hare edged forward and began nibbling the nuts, which encouraged Stephan to pick up a small rye loaf and take an experimental bite. It was bread that his mother had baked all his life but now it came as a new taste and, since it tasted good, he was soon devouring the loaf in hearty mouthfuls.

Eating contentedly, the hare moved closer. On its back was a bald patch and deep claw marks left by a wild cat. Stephan gently stroked the animal's silky ears and it looked at him with trusting brown eyes.

Stephan remained in the sanctary of the cave throughout the first day of his new life. Outside it rained continuously and, as the light faded, he was sitting cross-legged with the hare lying in his lap, watching the raindrops falling from the roof of the entrance. Had Josef and Marta seen their son in those quiet, peaceful moments they would have been greatly reassured. But they would have been deceived by his outward appearance. Inside, he was no longer the child they had known. He was closer to the animal lying in his lap, with only primitive instincts to guide him.

6

'Let's hope this is the right path.'

'Josef, don't worry. We'll find the cave.'

'The snow was that thick, I could hardly see in front of my nose.'

The two grey-haired men — the tall figure of Josef in the lead with the stocky figure of Petr a few paces behind — were toiling up a steep slope in a series of tight zig-zags. A fine drizzle was making the rocks slippery and, in spite of extra layers of sacking, they were both soaked to the skin. Each man carried a staff and a bundle of food slung over his back.

A week had passed since that desperate flight to the mountains — a week in which Josef and Marta had talked of little except Stephan and, even in moments of silence, their thoughts remained with him. Marta had wept a great deal and, more than once, Josef had been tempted to throw down his axe and go to see his son. But he had always been stopped by the knowledge that no one — except Petr — must ever learn their secret and, in any case, the only safe day to risk another visit would be Sunday, the day of rest.

Sunday brought not only the possibility of a journey to the mountains but also the intimidating prospect of morning Mass to be got through first. Dreading every moment of it, Josef and Marta appeared in church with bare heads and feet, with only coarse sackcloth tunics to cover their bodies.

They were made to stand throughout the service and, in full view of everyone, to listen to the unctuous priest castigating them in his sermon. When it was all over, they were treated like common felons or carriers of the plague. No one spoke to them — even people they had known all their lives turned away — and they were left to struggle home without a word of commiseration or encouragement.

It had been difficult for Petr to stand by and watch his

friends suffering these ordeals. But he was helpless to do anything except maintain a pretence of ignorance about the woodman's child while promising himself that he would visit them as soon as he could get away unnoticed. Later that morning he came knocking on the door to find Josef on the point of leaving and immediately offered to accompany him, saying, 'No one will suspect anything — not even my wife. I'm often out all day on a Sunday, seeing people.' So, with bundles of fresh provisions, they set out together.

Unaware of the imminent arrival of visitors, Stephan and the hare were happily playing in the cave. The boy was chasing the animal round and round and, though he was no match for the agile hare, he was laughing merrily. The wounds on the animal's back were almost healed and each time Stephan tried to grab it, the hare cheekily ducked out of his grasp.

Suddenly the animal pricked up its ears and turned to the entrance. Its trembling nose anxiously sniffed unfamiliar scents. The change in the alert little creature brought the boy to an abrupt halt and he stood listening with head cocked on one side. He could hear nothing above the roar of the waterfall, but the sensitive nose and acute hearing of the hare told it that strangers were near. It thumped with its hind legs on the floor and bolted to the rear of the cave. Stephan was about to follow when a distant shout made him hesitate.

'Stephan?' It was Josef calling from the bottom of the waterfall.

'Stephan?' There were two voices now, calling in unison.

The boy stood facing the entrance, puzzled by the unfamiliar sounds. He was used to the cries of the mountain animals and birds, but these sounds were different. In the pause which followed, he could hear the hare frantically thumping to him to come and hide.

Then the first voice called again, this time much nearer. Feeling suddenly afraid, he scooted away to join the hare in a narrow niche at the rear. Crouching in the darkness, he heard footsteps approach the entrance and an anxious voice calling in to the cave, 'Stephan, it's me — your father.'

He could feel the hare, which lay flattened against his legs, shivering with fright and as footsteps entered the cave, he too began to tremble.

'Perhaps this isn't the right cave,' the other voice was saying.

'I'm sure it is. Here's the blankets and the shawl I carried him in. And here's the cloth the food was wrapped in.'

'Well, he's obviously eaten it all.'

'But where is he? Why isn't he here?'

'He's gone out, that's all.'

'In this weather?'

'Why not? You've complained often enough in the past about him being out in all weathers.'

'That was the forest. Here it's different. He could have fallen.'

'Josef, my friend, you mustn't alarm yourself like this. I'm sure the boy is safe.'

'But I want to see him — to be sure.'

Footsteps receded from the cave and the voice called outside, 'Stephan? *Stephan?*'

'I don't like it, Petr,' the voice said, coming back in the cave. 'I don't like it at all.'

'Perhaps, it's better this way.'

'Better?'

'Well, perhaps it's better if we just leave the food and go. That way you won't upset the boy, or yourself. Come. Let's get these bundles off our backs.'

There were rustling sounds and two dull thuds of parcels being dropped on the floor. Then muffled footsteps slowly approached the rear of the cave. Wide-eyed in the darkness, Stephan could sense a tall figure looming towards him and he pressed tighter in against the rocks.

'Stephan?' a quiet, troubled voice called into the darkness.

'It's no good,' the other voice said from the front of the cave. 'The boy isn't here. We must start for home while it's still light.'

The tall figure was now so close to Stephan that he could hear it breathing.

At that moment, only a few feet of darkness separated father and son. But, in so many other ways, a great gulf divided them. And even if the man had discovered the boy, he would not have found the son he knew, for the child squeezed against the rock recognized only an instinct which said, you are a stranger and I am afraid.

The figure gave a deep sigh and shuffling footsteps receded towards the entrance.

'You were hardly likely to find him in there,' the practical voice said. 'You'll see him next Sunday.'

'I'd like to see him now.'

'I know. But we must hurry. It soon gets dark this time of year.'

Footsteps retreated from the cave and were drowned by the thundering water. In their dark hiding place, the boy and the hare waited until it seemed safe to move then, cautiously, Stephan limped forward, blinking in the light, while the hare confidently hopped ahead to sniff the tempting bundles.

7

Hans sat brooding in front of the fire. Wrapped in a torn sheepskin rug with his thick muscular arms folded across his chest, he stared moodily at the spluttering wood. The first real snow of winter had been falling since mid-day and it was coming in through the hole in the roof.

Behind him on a bare wooden table, a solitary rush dip cast deep shadows on his wife's pale cheeks and sunken eyes. She sat in weary silence, looking into the yellow light.

On the floor, other younger faces were touched by the flickering light — a dark-haired boy of thirteen who helped his father in the smithy, and two younger girls who sat huddled together for warmth. One of them coughed at regular intervals. In a dark corner on a straw pallet, a small boy slept fitfully under coarse blankets. No one spoke. Only the sizzling fire and the dry, rasping coughs interrupted the silence.

It was a week before the Feast of St Nicholas and Hans could not shrug off the feeling that he had been cheated. It had been rumbling around inside him for weeks and, as he thought of it now, he kicked angrily at a piece of wood that had fallen from the fire.

He had heard the woodman's child declared to be a creature of the Devil; he had watched the parents making penance on three occasions in church. But none of it seemed enough. He still felt cheated. Above all, he felt cheated by Petr.

His feud with the miller was long-standing. It had begun in childhood when Petr refused to be frightened by his bullying manner and took the lead. When, many years later, Petr had been elected headman in preference to himself it only served to fuel the resentment and hostility he had felt for a long time.

So far he had done nothing except vent his anger on his family, making his wife miserable and his children afraid. But that afternoon a peasant farmer had brought a horse in for shoeing and casually joked that at least they couldn't blame the cripple for the snow that had just begun to fall, and Hans resolved to put an end to the feelings that were torturing him. He dispatched his son with messages for Vislav and Lobvic and now he was waiting for them to answer his summons.

They arrived promptly, and together. At their knock, Hans quickly moved to open the door. They were standing ankle deep in snow and he beckoned them inside, closing the door behind them to shut out the draught of cold air whistling round the smoke-filled room.

'A vile night, neighbour,' Vislav muttered, shaking the snow from his sacking cape and stamping his feet.

'Get yourselves warm by the fire,' Hans replied with rough hospitality.

Briefly nodding to the blacksmith's wife, the two visitors sat themselves down on the stools already set for them and held their hands to the fire. The children on the floor watched them in silence.

Hans poured three tots of rye spirit into small earthenware beakers and handed them round.

'For turning out on such a foul night,' he said.

'Your boy said it was urgent,' Vislav remarked grudgingly.

'And so it is.'

'We wouldn't do it for many men,' Lobvic said with a sniff.

The blacksmith grunted and, for a moment or two, they drank in silence. Then, in a sudden outburst, he said, 'We've been made to look like fools.'

The others looked at him in surprise.

'How d'you mean, Hans?' Vislav asked warily.

'It's the miller. He's the one that's done it.'

At the mention of Petr, the others shifted uneasily.

'How do you mean, Hans?' the weedy carpenter repeated.

'It strikes me it was very convenient the cripple was taken away when he was.'

Lobvic crossed himself and looked thoughtful.

'What're you getting at?' Vislav asked, thoroughly confused.

'It's very simple. That story of the flying creature got a lot of people out of a lot of trouble.'

Lobvic quickly crossed himself again.

'Are you suggesting it isn't true?' he asked cautiously.

'All I'm saying is that we don't know for certain if it's true.'

'But if the child wasn't taken by the Devil, where is he?' Vislav demanded with a scowl.

'In hiding of course.'

This new possibility silenced the visitors for a while. Then, the carpenter, whose mind was sharper than that of the man sitting beside him, shook his head and sniffed.

'But the woodman wasn't at the meeting,' he said. 'Nor was his wife. How could they know what we were going to do?'

'Exactly! How did they know? I'll tell you, my friends.'

Hans leaned forward with the air of a man about to reveal the answer to a great mystery. 'They knew because someone told them.'

'Told them?' Vislav asked, trying to grapple with the idea. 'But who?'

'Think, man. Think back to the meeting. Who was it who stopped us going for the child there and then? Who was it who made us go to the castle and refused to come with us?'

The answer was so self-evident that it hardly needed to be voiced. But —

'Petr!' Vislav triumphantly exclaimed.

'Petr,' Lobvic mused, scratching his long nose.

'Petr,' Hans growled. 'It *has* to be him. No one else would have dared to do it. And that's not all.' The others looked expectantly at him. 'I believe he put the woodman up to the whole story. That clod wouldn't have the wit to think of it himself.'

'His wife might,' the carpenter, who had always fancied Marta, said.

'I tell you, it was the miller's work.'

'You're right, neighbour,' Vislav emphatically declared. 'We've been made fools of, and it's all down to the miller.' The coarse skin on his face was flushed with anger. 'I'd like to get my hands on him.'

'And so you may,' the blacksmith replied with a hoarse chuckle.

'How's that then?'

'Simple. Even the Devil's child has to eat. We find out when they take him food and then we follow them. Once we know where the cripple is hidden, we'll go to the Lord.'

'Easier said than done,' Lobvic sniffed.

'I tell you, it'll be easy.' Hans grinned at the carpenter. 'You know the woodman best. Make friends with him. Say you're sorry about the child. Mark my words, it won't be long before he gives himself away.'

'Supposing he doesn't tell me anything?'

'Then you'll have made yourself a new friend.'

Vislav guffawed loudly at the look of prim distaste on the carpenter's face.

'But what if Lobvic's right? What if he doesn't find out anything?'

'It won't be the end of the world. Remember, it's not the cripple who made fools of us — it's the miller. And there's another way we can get at him.'

'How?'

'By spreading rumours about him. We'll say he's dishonest. Not fit to be headman any more.'

'But suppose they don't believe it?'

'When you're starving, my friend, you'll believe anything.'

8

'We-e-e-e-e!' Stephan squealed, sliding down a steep, snow-covered slope with arms and legs in the air. Behind him, the hare concentrated on holding a steady course.

Half way down, the boy gleefully abandoned all attempts at control and rolled head over heels, throwing up such a cloud of snow that the small animal could do nothing but tuck itself into a furry ball and blindly roll down the slope until it joined the boy in a breathless heap in a snowdrift at the bottom.

Laughing and panting, Stephan blew the snow from his face and waded out of the drift, while the hare shook the snow from its fur. Without delay, the boy eagerly began to toil up the slope again with his small companion lightly hopping on ahead.

It was a rare winter's day of bright sunshine with every ledge and crevasse covered in dazzling snow and a clear, gentian blue sky overhead. For once, even the highest peaks were visible — finely chizzled outlines of white against blue.

By the time Stephan reached the top, he was sweating profusely and he wiped his face with a careless sweep of an arm. Living in the mountains, out in all weathers, his skin had toughened and tanned to the colour of a ripe chestnut. His hair was now a tangled, golden mane and as he stood, hands on hips, in torn, dirty clothes, there was a recklessness and abandonment about him which made him look the wild creature that he was.

His hazel eyes quickly scanned the vista below him. The forest trees were capped with snow and, had he but known, the dark smudges in the far distance on the white tablecloth of the plain were the castle and village of Bletz. But they meant nothing to him, aroused no curiosity. His only contact with the world of men was the frightening creature who regularly brought food to the cave and who sent him scuttling away into hiding. Unwittingly, he had sent his father away each week bitterly disappointed, with only the knowledge that the last consignment of food had been eaten to reassure him that his son was still alive.

Stephan sat down and pushed himself on to the slope, squealing with delight as he gathered speed and plunged head first into the snowdrift. Helpless with laughter, he shook the snow from his face and hair and looked round for the hare, confidently expecting it to have followed. But the wise little creature was still at the top, waiting for the cloud of snow to settle.

Standing with snow up to his knees, the boy excitedly whistled to the pert white form at the top. The animal gingerly stepped on to the slope and, with a gentle push of its hind legs, began a steady toboggan run downhill.

They were so intent on their innocent sport that neither of them was aware of being watched by two dark predatory eyes. Several hundred feet above them, in an ocean of blue, the stately progress of the hare was being studied by a golden eagle — a bird of huge proportions that was stronger and could fly further and faster than any other bird in the mountains. It had been attracted by the movement on the slope — dark shadows on the snow — and now it assessed the hare's speed with cold detachment.

At the bottom of the slope, Stephan whistled encouragingly to his companion. High above, the mighty eagle lazily rolled over and began its deadly power dive.

With happy gurgling noises, the boy knelt in the snow, holding out his arms to receive the small animal steadily sliding towards him. Still at a great height, the bird was travelling so fast that its body made a high-pitched whining sound as it hurtled through the air. Wings flat to its body, head and neck craned forward, it was a perfect streamlined shape racing towards the earth.

Only two yards separated the hare and Stephan's outstretched arms when, too late, they heard the noise in the sky. The boy was buffeted off balance by the sudden rush of wind. The animal, which had survived the attack of a wild cat, had no chance of avoiding the outstretched talons. Its end was swift and inevitable.

Stephan screamed at the monster bird, throwing himself at it with flailing fists — only to be beaten off with a casual flap of its wings. He struggled up and, with tears streaming down his face, he attacked the predator again — and again he was thrust aside with cruel indifference. For a third time he hurled himself at the bird trying to reach the small creature lying dead under its talons. With an angry shriek and one disdainful blow of its wings, the eagle knocked him senseless.

He emerged from the black void of unconsciousness with the uncomfortable sensations of wind and hair whipping across his face. At the same time, he felt he was falling and instinctively reached out to steady himself. But he failed to make contact with anything tangible. The pressure round his waist which, at first, was dimly felt as an inexplicable constriction, now became so tight and painful that it made him gasp for breath. Jolted into full consciousness, he opened his eyes and, as his vision cleared, he cried out in alarm for he thought he could see rocks and ravines far below and a mountain cliff flashing by in a dizzy blur. In a panic, he struggled and twisted in the vice-like grip round his waist to find a brown-feathered body just above his head and two huge outstretched wings, quite motionless except for the very tips which fluttered in the breeze.

In a sickening, terrifying flash, he realized that he was dangling in space, carried face downwards by the giant bird — and falling. The rocks rushing up to meet him were evidence of that. Wildly thrashing the air and screaming, his one thought was to escape the talons round his waist. But the eagle took no notice and continued on its downward glide.

Suddenly, the powerful wings sprang into action, beating the air with a thunderous noise to check the speed of their descent. Then they gently parachuted down beside a sheer wall of rock and, a few moments later, without warning, the talons released their grip and Stephan helplessly fell under his own weight to land on a pile of dried heather and twigs.

The fall had been no more than two feet and had happened so unexpectedly that Stephan had no time to cry out. It was only as he lay huddled on the eagle's nest in a state of severe shock that he began to scream with fright. Unmoved, the eagle calmly shook its feathers back into place.

It took Stephan a long time to recover sufficiently to raise his head and look round. He found to his horror that he was on a narrow ledge with a massive wall of rock behind him and a sheer drop in front. The foul stench of rotting remains of the eagle's prey made him choke. Driven by a blind urge to escape, he half got to his feet and lurched towards the edge. The eagle immediately sprang into action, squawking in a bleak, harsh voice and flapping its wings to keep him back. Stephan fought even harder, but he was no match for the relentless wings and at last he gave up and collapsed, crying, on the nest.

Slowly, as the day progressed, the weather changed and by late afternoon a sharp wind was blowing across the ledge and the sky was filled with clouds. The boy whimpered piteously with the cold and grief for the hare. He gathered his torn garments about him, abjectly longing for the warmth and shelter of the cave.

The eagle regarded him critically through stern, uncompromising eyes. Then it sidled along the ledge, making dry creaking sounds. The boy cringed away in fear. But punishment was not in the bird's mind. It stretched out a wing and enveloped him in a warm canopy of feathers. It was not a kindly gesture in a human sense but was prompted by practical necessity, as though some instinct told the bird that the small creature needed protection if it was to survive a night on the exposed ledge.

Drawing up its neck and opening its beak wide, the eagle emitted a deafening shriek that made the boy tremble. He had no way of knowing that the bird was warning the other mountain creatures that the child was his — and his alone.

9

Darkness crept over the mountains like a powerful liquid that has the property of dissolving massive rocks into insubstantial space. Only the rock beneath Stephan's body felt solid and secure, the rest was a black void.

For a long time, he lay huddled beneath the eagle's wing too frightened to move. A howling wind lashed the cliff, making their position seem so precarious that each time he felt the bird buffeted by the gale, he was sure they would be blown from the ledge and he would fall to the rocks below. But, like a brave mariner keeping watch, the eagle boldly faced the wind and flurries of snow, refusing to be dislodged from its perch.

As the hours passed, Stephan's terror slowly subsided. In spite of all that had happened, he began to feel grateful for the warmth of the eagle's body, for its strength and indomitable will. In the early hours of the morning he fell into a fitful sleep.

With the faint grey streaks of dawn the wind dropped and, for the first time, the eagle eased its cramped muscles and shook the snow from its feathers. It lifted its wing and looked with interest at the small figure huddled on the nest. Stephan stirred but did not wake. The bird gave an impatient squawk, folded its wing and hopped a pace away. Stephan woke with a start and, remembering where he was, gave a cry of alarm. The eagle preened its feathers, unmoved by the shouts of protest coming from the nest.

Shivering with the cold, with his knees clasped to his chest, Stephan was staring bleakly across the yawning abyss when a sudden miraculous transformation in the scene before him made him forget his wretchedness. The sun had just risen above the mountain peaks and was flooding the landscape with shafts of golden light. Below him, the mist hanging over the lower slopes was ablaze with every colour of the rainbow. It was like watching the creation of the world.

For several minutes, Stephan was transfixed by this elemental drama. Then, glancing at the eagle, he was met by another awesome sight. Caught in a shaft of light, with its wings folded round its body in a rich mantle of feathers and its proud neck crowned with a golden head, the great bird stood like an absolute monarch surveying its domain.

Sensing the boy looking at it, the eagle gave him an imperious stare. With an abrupt squawk, it leaped from the ledge and glided effortlessly into space. Stephan was on his feet at once shouting to it to return. The bird screeched short-temperedly but dropped a wing and circled back, flying so close to the boy that a wing tip brushed his face, toppling him back on the nest. Stay there! it screeched without pausing in its flight and with slow measured beats, it flew off across the mountains.

Earthbound, Stephan watched the bird until it was no more than a dark speck that finally disappeared in the far distance. He kicked aimlessly at a loose stone with his good foot and it fell silently into the abyss below. He felt very alone, very vulnerable — and very cold.

He was still huddled on the nest when some time later he heard beating wings overhead. He looked up to see the eagle swooping down towards him and, in a few moments, it landed expertly on the ledge. In its beak was the limp form of a dead vole. He watched the bird pin down the creature in its talons and rip open the fur with its beak. Then, it moved towards him with a morsel of flesh in its beak. Stephan recoiled in horror.

Puzzled, the bird moved closer, making odd little creaking sounds. Stephan cried out in protest, turning away and waving his arms. But the bird continued to advance until the meat was pressed against his face. In desperation, he scrambled to his feet and retreated along the ledge, pursued by the eagle.

Suddenly, as he took a step backwards, his foot landed on empty air. Wildly, he grabbed at the rocks. But they were already out of reach. In a flash, the eagle threw itself from the ledge and dived after him.

With talons already open it reached for the falling body, but only managed to rip the boy's clothes. The wings thrashed the air, trying to catch up with the boy who was plunging down like a stone. The talons grabbed again. And again. And finally secured themselves round the boy's waist. Now, the wings thrashed, fighting for control. But they could not check the falling dead weight, and eagle and boy dived together in a steeply curved arc, with the air screaming past their faces.

Still the rocks raced up to meet them as the eagle fought for mastery. At the lowest point in the arc, it braced its back and, with mighty beats of its wings, it pulled them back from the dive and into a swooping upward path. The sudden change of direction sent the blood rushing from Stephan's head to his stomach, and he almost lost consciousness.

It had all happened so quickly there had been no time to breath, but as the climb continued and he was able to appreciate that he was out of danger, he gulped a mouthful of air and let it out in a cry that went echoing round the crags. It was nothing short of a miracle. One moment pulled by gravity to certain death; the next, hauled to safety by the colossal strength of the eagle.

The climb gradually levelled out and soon they were gliding round in a wide circle. Stephan trembled uncontrollably — an involuntary reaction to his fall — but this meant little to him compared to the joy he now felt of floating in the air, defying the pull of the earth. It was like being transported into the most perfect dream. It was all so smooth, quiet, graceful and effortless.

In his ecstasy, Stephan hardly noticed the eagle hovering over the ledge. But when he was dropped on the spiky nest, he was brought back to reality with an abrupt, painful bump.

The bird squawked disapprovingly and coolly shook its feathers into place. Stephan's face crumpled and he began to cry. Stop it! the bird rasped, as remote and stern as ever. The boy bit his lip as he tried to hold back his tears.

For a long time neither of them moved. Having rescued its captive the bird seemed to lose all interest in him. It was bewildering and frustrating for Stephan, who had been shown a world he never knew existed — a world in which he was no longer handicapped by the weight of his clubbed foot and the uneven lengths of his legs, which made him sway and contort his body even when walking slowly. Those brief, heady moments of flight had been like chains falling from a prisoner. He knew now what it was like to be a free-floating spirit of the air — and nothing could equal that.

He glanced nervously at the eagle as it dozed in the pale sunlight, no longer a figure of majesty but an untidy mess of ruffled feathers. With the timidity of a child plucking up enough courage to speak to an august father, Stephan attempted a hesitant caw. The bird opened one eye and regarded him with new interest. He cawed again, with more confidence, and the proud head slightly lifted as though deigning to accept the compliment.

Encouraged, Stephan sat up with a straight back and a brave tilt to his head. With legs crossed and arms folded, he quietly watched the shifting patterns of sunlight and shadow drifting across the mountain sides.

10

The unexpected banging on the door made Josef and Marta start. It caught them in the middle of preparations for another visit to the cave — Josef was binding his legs with straw and Marta had a griddle pan full of small rye loaves on the fire. They looked at each other in alarm and then, with urgent gestures, the woodman waved to his wife to clear the table of provisions waiting to be packed, while he gathered up the remains of the straw and dumped them in a corner. Marta anxiously pointed to the griddle pan. With a helpless shrug, Josef shook his head. He quickly glanced round the room and moved to open the door.

'I was beginning to think no one was in,' the visitor said with a smirk.

Josef's heart sank at the sight of the carpenter.

'I've come to see how you're getting on,' the man continued, trying to look past the woodman and rather obviously sniffing at the smells coming from inside. 'Is your wife cooking?' he asked.

'For Christmas,' Josef grunted.

'She was always a good housewife,' Lobvic said, taking a step forward and forcing Josef either to give way or to be deliberately discourteous.

'Good day, Marta,' the man said, strolling into the room.

'Good day, Lobvic,' she replied nervously.

'Busy I see,' he said, making himself at home and examining the contents of the griddle pan. 'You've enough loaves there for *two* families.'

'My husband has a big appetite,' she said.

'I wish I had. But it's just as well I don't — not with my family.'

The couple laughed dutifully. The way the man's eyes kept darting about the room was making them both very uneasy.

'It seems I came just in time,' the visitor said, nodding at the straw leggings.

'There's a fallen tree needs lopping,' Josef muttered.

The visitor sniffed and turned to Marta. 'And how are you, my good woman? We see you so rarely in the village — except at morning Mass.'

'We live very quietly,' she replied in a subdued voice.

'Of course, of course. Quite understandable. Well, I mustn't keep you from your cooking or you, neighbour, from your labours — unless you'd like company?'

Josef tried not to look rattled. 'Er — no,' he said searching for an excuse. 'It's a long way from here — and the tree's fallen in brambles.'

'Well in that case . . .' the carpenter nodded. 'And I should be getting back. Family duties.'

'Of course,' Josef mumbled.

The visitor made a move towards the door. 'God be with you, Marta,' he said sanctimoniously.

'And with you, sir.'

'And don't forget, if your husband doesn't eat all those loaves, I've got seven mouths to feed at home.'

'Goodness me,' Marta said, sounding suitably surprised.

Chuckling to himself, Lobvic strolled with maddening slowness to the door which Josef held open for him.

'God be with you, neighbour,' he said, stepping outside at last.

'And with you,' Josef replied, attempting a smile.

With an airy wave, the visitor stalked away under the wary gaze of the woodman who remained at the door until the carpenter disappeared behind the oak trees. He closed the door with a bang.

'What did he want?' Marta asked anxiously.

Josef shook his head.

'Do be careful, husband. Perhaps you should stay at home today.'

56

'And leave our son short of food? I'm not going to let *him* stop me.'

His determination was understandable. But if he had not felt so angry at the carpenter's intrusion, he might have paused to reflect on the possibility of his departure being observed by Lobvic — as indeed it was.

Hearing the door bang, the carpenter quickly doubled back to hide behind the broad trunk of an oak tree and, a little later, he was rewarded with the sight of Josef leaving the dwelling, well wrapped in sacking and carrying a tell-tale bundle on his back. Too elated with his discovery to bother with following the woodman, Lobvic ran back to Bletz as fast as his spindly legs would carry him to report his news to Hans.

Later that same day, after the evening service, the black-smith lost no time in using the information to his own advantage. He waited in the shadows at the rear of the church until the rest of the congregation had filed out, then he quietly approached the priest who was clearing up at the altar by the light of two tall candles.

'Father, I must speak to you,' he said.

The priest was visibly startled and wheeled round to see who was addressing him. When he saw Hans at the altar rail, he drew himself up and with a dismissive wave said, 'Another time.'

'I think you should hear what I have to say — now,' the blacksmith growled.

Father Vilem hesitated. Then, with a condescending sigh, he said, 'Very well. If it is urgent.'

Hans grinned. 'The woodman is taking food to the cripple,' he announced, coming straight to the point.

As a past master in the art of concealment, Father Vilem received the news without the flicker of an eyelid. 'Wood-man? Cripple? What are you talking about?

'You know well enough what I'm talking about. The Devil's child.'

'How do you know this?' the priest asked with a casualness that even Hans had to admire.

'That would be telling, wouldn't it?'

'In that case, you can hardly expect me to believe it,' Father Vilem retorted, firmly turning his back on the blacksmith and resuming his duties at the altar.

It almost fooled Hans, who stood for a moment unsure of his ground, silently cursing the carpenter for not returning with more evidence.

'I think the Lord of Bletz will believe it,' he said belligerently, and turned to the door.

'Wait!'

Hans drew to a leisurely halt.

'Why are you telling me this?'

It was the blacksmith's turn to look innocent. 'I thought you'd be interested. After all, you were the one who agreed with the woodman. You know, that story about his child being carried away by a flying creature. The Devil, I think you said. Now, it seems you were wrong.'

Father Vilem looked at Hans' arrogant, grinning face and, for the first time, he was unable to keep a note of strain from his voice.

'Who else knows this?' he demanded sharply.

The blacksmith was in no hurry to reply and ambled back to the priest.

'Who else knows this?' the priest repeated.

Hans shrugged. 'Only myself — and the man who told me,' he said.

'And no one else must know. I order you as your priest.'

Hans thought for a moment, then gave a loud guffaw.

'It won't do, Father. It won't do at all.'

'What do you mean, it won't do?' Beads of perspiration on Father Vilem's blotchy face were caught in the flickering light of the candles.

'I'm an honest man, Father — and can keep a secret. But I can't speak for the other man, can I?'

'Then let me speak to him.'

'I can't do that, Father. I promised I wouldn't give his name and I can't break a promise. Mind you, if I had, say, a position in Bletz, I could make him keep silent. What I need is — how shall I put it? — more authority.'

Father Vilem studied the blacksmith in silence. Then his fat belly began to shake beneath his black habit and he roared with laughter.

'You're not only a rogue, blacksmith — you're an ambitious rogue.'

'I knew you'd understand.'

Without more ado, the priest stepped down from the altar and waddled to the wooden stand on which was chained a large Bible.

'I'll help you,' he said decisively, 'on three conditions. First, you will swear on this sacred book that what you have told me is true. Second, you will swear before Almighty God that you will tell no one else about this — '

'Now, wait a minute . . . ,' Hans began.

'And third,' the priest continued, overriding the interruption, 'with your hand on this book, you will give me the name of your informant.'

Hans glowered at the priest, rubbing his mouth with the back of a clenched fist.

'How do I know you'll help me?' he asked warily.

'You'll just have to trust me,' the priest cheerfully replied. 'Well?'

Hans grimly nodded and approached Father Vilem who grabbed his hand and firmly placed it on the Bible before he could change his mind.

'I swear by this holy book,' the priest began at once.

'I swear by this holy book,' the blacksmith heard himself repeating, with his mind on the future.

11

The ledge was already in shadow when the eagle woke from its customary doze. It shook its feathers and looked at the boy who had not left the ledge since his near fatal fall on the morning after his arrival. He was shivering with the cold but sitting straightbacked, determined not to complain. The bird seemed to approve of this, for there was a satisfied gleam in its dark eyes as it sidled across the ledge and pecked at the boy's clothes.

Stephan did his best not to flinch, but when the eagle gave an impatient squawk, he hid his face in his hands. He was even more alarmed when, without warning, the bird flapped its wings and lightly hopped on to his shoulders. He felt the talons tightly grip him under his arms, heard the wings flap again and, suddenly, he was being lifted from the nest. He cried out and grabbed at some twigs. Then his heart gave a great leap —far from meaning to hurt him, the eagle was answering his deepest longings. They were flying again. *Flying*.

Hanging beneath the eagle as it circled round, searching for an up-current of air, Stephan gave an exultant shout. Then quite unexpectedly, as he looked down, his confidence vanished. In a panic he reached up and grabbed the bird's legs. The angry screeches that followed and the uneven flapping of its wings made Stephan fear it would turn back. Cautiously he let go of the legs, which drew immediate approval from the bird and, with powerful movements of its wings, it climbed into the sky.

With his heart in his mouth, Stephan tried to concentrate on the stately rhythm of the huge wings rising and falling and, after a while, this unfaltering movement set up an echo in his own body. He found he could breathe in time to the rise and fall of the wings. Dangling in space, trusting in the eagle's mastery of the air, Stephan gave himself over to the unending marvels of that evening flight.

For mile after mile they flew over the mountains — sometimes, up with the clouds; sometimes, swooping into a dark valley. They raced across snow-covered slopes, flying so close to the ground that Stephan's feet skidded through the soft snow. Wheeling, gliding, twisting, turning on the ever-changing currents of air.

Laughing, crying, holding his breath as the blood rushed to his head, gasping as it lurched to his stomach. It was the most thrilling, frightening journey imaginable.

It was on one of their swooping dives that Stephan saw a torrent of water cascading over a high cliff which he recognized immediately as the waterfall by the cave. Excitedly he grabbed one of the eagle's legs and shouted to the bird to dive closer. Surprisingly, it obediently dipped a wing to take them skimming across the pool at the bottom. With a face wet with spray, Stephan urged the bird to climb and, again without protest, it spiralled upwards. He could see the cave now and, as he called to the bird to land, it abruptly released its grip and he fell in a breathless heap on the ground.

Still giddy from the flight, Stephan picked himself up and hobbled to the entrance. The eagle watched his movements with stern concentration.

In the dim light inside, Stephan saw all the familiar objects on the floor — blankets, sheepskin rug and a fresh bundle of food. The sight of the food made him feel ravenously hungry and he tugged at the knots to open the bundle. He was stopped by an imperious squawk and he turned to see the eagle in the entrance. The bird squawked again and flapped its wings, impatient to be gone. But Stephan was in no hurry to leave —at least, not before he had eaten.

This is my food, he squawked, holding out a rye loaf and taking a hearty mouthful. The eagle was not amused and tossed its golden head. Come! it screeched.

Reluctantly, Stephan threw away the remains of the loaf and moved to obey. Then he froze. His heart was beating quickly and he stared open-mouthed at the bird. He had suddenly realized that he was not the eagle's prisoner any more. He had only to hide at the back of the cave, out of reach of the bird, and he need never return to that cold, lofty prison on the ledge. In a wild scramble, he grabbed the sack of provisions and hobbled away into the darkness.

At this the eagle screeched with fury, strutting into the cave and beating its wings. Undaunted, the boy wormed his way into a narrow passage where he knew the bird could not follow.

Come! the eagle shrieked with frightening power.

In the darkness, Stephan anxiously listened for sounds of the eagle's approach. But the bird seemed unwilling to venture further into the cave. For a while, there was silence between them. Then, with a screech, the eagle left the cave and flew off.

Stephan limped from his hiding place and settled on a blanket to eat. Then a new thought came to him, which put all thought of food from his mind. If he let the eagle go, he would never fly again. He would be doomed once more to drag himself over the ground. Was the peace and shelter of the cave — a lonely place without the hare — worth more than the freedom of the air? With a cry, he dashed from the cave and feverishly searched the darkening sky.

The eagle was quickly climbing. In a few moments it would be gone. Stephan yelled and yelled until there were tears streaming down his face. Then, just as he was giving up hope, he saw the wings falter. He waited with bated breath for the wings to dip and, to his great joy, he saw the bird roll over.

He was laughing and waving as the eagle came swooping down, flying so low that he was sent reeling backwards. Without pause, it climbed in the sky, wheeled about and dived at him again, screeching angrily as it passed overhead, then upwards into the sky. For a third time, it came swooping down, heading straight at the boy who crouched on the ground with his head in his hands. But at the last moment, it coolly flicked its wings and landed majestically on the rocks beside him.

Come! it screeched and, shakily, Stephan rose to obey. Then, remembering the food and blankets and braving the eagle's fury, he dashed into the cave and emerged almost at once clutching these comforts from his old home. In a few moments, they were airborne once more and though he knew he would never live in the cave again, Stephan's heart was singing as they flew over the mountains.

It was almost dark by the time they reached the ledge. The familiar night winds were howling across the cliff face and Stephan gratefully wrapped himself in a blanket as he settled down on the nest. The eagle stretched out a wing and he nestled against its warm body under the shelter of its feathers.

Like a proud sentry, the bird prepared for another night of vigil. With great pride it shrieked, he came back because he wanted to!

12

E ven before he entered the cave, Josef knew there was something wrong from the absence of footprints in the freshly fallen snow. He hurried inside and was met by an even more alarming sight. The floor was bare — blankets, remains of food had all gone. He stood for a moment, not knowing what to do. Then he dropped the sack of provisions and ran outside to search the neighbouring slopes, calling for Stephan until oncoming darkness forced him to return home.

He and Marta spent the evening consumed with anxious thoughts which prompted many questions, but no answers. They retired to bed comforted only by the knowledge that in the morning Josef would seek Petr's advice.

They woke to find there had been a heavy fall of snow — drifts lay banked against the hut and rows of icicles hung from the eaves. Undeterred, Josef set out with courage restored, his warm breath steaming in the frosty air.

The mill stood on the edge of Bletz beside the river and, having no wish to meet anyone, he chose a route that skirted the village. In the distance, he could see trails of smoke lazily rising in the mist and small dark figures clearing snow from their dwellings.

As he approached the mill he heard bangs and cracking noises of someone attacking the ice. It was Petr trying to clear the large wooden waterwheel.

'Look at this,' the miller complained. 'No sooner do I clear one paddle than the rest have frozen up again.' He tossed aside the metal bar he had been using as an ice-breaker. 'The Lord'll just have to wait for his flour this morning — and that's all there is to it.' He blew on his hands to get them warm. 'What brings you here, old friend?'

'It's about Stephan . . .' Josef began.

'Not so loud,' Petr interrupted. 'There are eyes and ears everywhere. Come inside the mill.'

They walked together from the dazzling brightness of the snow into a dimly lit interior where everything was coated in a fine film of flour dust — the floor, the timbers of the roof and the two massive stone wheels that lay waiting to be fed with the sacks of grain piled against a wall.

'The Lord doesn't go without,' Josef grunted.

'It makes me sick,' Petr snorted, 'to see one man with so much and the rest of us hungry.'

'I'd be tempted to take some for myself.'

'And so am I — often. But it'd be more than my life's worth. Besides, there are usually two soldiers here when the mill's working. They went away this morning when they saw the river had frozen. But no doubt they'll return. So let's not waste any more time. Tell me about Stephan.'

Briefly, Josef described his disturbing visit to the cave. When he finished, Petr thought for a moment, then said, 'I understand your worry, but it's my belief the boy has found another cave. Everything points to that. By now he'll know his stretch of the mountains like the back of his hand and it's not surprising if he's found a better place to shelter. But if you're still not convinced, why don't I go with you next Sunday? With two of us looking we'll soon track him down.'

Josef smiled gratefully. 'You're a good friend,' he said.

'Think nothing of it. I shall enjoy the walk.'

They shook hands warmly and walked together towards the door. They were about to step outside when distant shouting made them stop. The miller put out a hand to restrain the woodman as a crowd of men, brandishing sticks, came striding across the snow-bound meadow. One voice was raised above the rest.

'What's going on?' Josef asked.

The miller shook his head and quickly closed the door,

barring it with a heavy beam. A moment later, a snowball crashed against the wooden wall of the mill. From the noise it made it clearly concealed a stone.

'Down with the traitor!' an angry voice yelled.

'Vislav,' the miller said under his breath.

This was followed by a barrage of stones and snowballs that came thudding against the walls, splintering the wood. And more voices yelling, 'Down with the traitor!'

The two men inside listened with growing alarm to the pandemonium outside. Then they heard the blacksmith's voice raised above the rest.

'We know you're in there, miller,' he bellowed.

Josef looked in horror at his friend who was facing the barred door with hands clenched in anger.

'Miller!' the blacksmith yelled.

'I'm here,' Petr replied in a steady voice.

'Then come on out. Or do we have to come for you?'

'This mill is the property of the Lord of Bletz. You know well enough what will happen if you damage it.'

'Then come out. Stop hiding behind the Lord like you always do.'

This drew wild laughter and more abuse from the rabble.

Josef saw Petr take a step towards the door and he grabbed his friend's arm.

'No,' Petr whispered, trying to break free.

'But they might hurt you.'

'Better me than the mill. I must speak to them before they do anything foolish.'

'Miller,' the blacksmith was shouting. 'This is your last chance.'

'Please, let me go,' Petr urged in a desperate whisper. 'I *must* speak to them. But keep well back. They mustn't know you're here. I beg you, let go of my arm.'

Josef could do nothing but obey and, with an appalling sense of impotence, he hung back in the shadows while Petr removed the wooden bar and opened the door.

'That's better,' Hans jeered. 'You've done the wise thing after all — headman.'

The heavy sarcasm in his voice made Josef bristle with anger.

'You should all be at work,' Petr said, sternly addressing the crowd which contained most of the men of the village.

'You can't scare us,' Vislav shouted, waving a long stick.

'We're not the guilty ones,' Hans jeered.

'Traitor!' Vislav yelled, encouraging the others to join with him.

'For your own good,' Petr cried, valiantly trying to make himself heard above the din, 'go back to work. Don't be misled by this man. He's leading you into great danger.'

'You're the one in danger,' Hans yelled. 'You're the one accused.'

The rabble noisily agreed.

'We know what you're up to,' the blacksmith thundered on. 'Feathering your own nest while the rest of us starve.'

'What am I accused of?' Petr demanded, his voice full of anger. 'What's this "feathering of the nest" that you speak of? Speak plainly and I'll truthfully answer any charge you make. I've nothing to hide.'

He spoke with such honest conviction that some of the men began to feel uneasy. They had been whipped into a frenzy by the rumours spread about by Hans and his cronies during the past few days and had set out determined to see the miller punished. They waited for the blacksmith to speak. But before Hans could reply there was a new sound which struck fear in many hearts. As one man, the crowd turned to see a troop of horsemen riding down on them at full gallop, churning up a cloud of snow. Some of the peasants threw down their sticks and ran for their lives, the rest stood like panic-stricken sheep as the soldiers circled them, swords already drawn.

The captain of the troop rode straight to Petr.

'What's the meaning of this, headman?' he demanded.

'A foolish argument,' the miller replied, trying to make light of the demonstration. 'A misunderstanding — nothing more. They were just on their way back to work.'

The soldier hesitated but seemed prepared to accept the miller's explanation. But a peaceful end to the matter was not part of the blacksmith's plan. He had always known the demonstration would bring soldiers on the scene — that was part of the plan — and now that they were there he was not going to see them go away empty-handed.

'That's not it at all,' he shouted. 'The miller's lying, as usual.'

'Who are you?' the captain barked.

'Hans, the blacksmith. And I'll tell you, honestly, why we're here. We came to accuse the miller of certain crimes — crimes against us, and against the Lord of Bletz.'

'What crimes?'

'Stealing the Lord's grain.'

The words sent a sudden chill through Petr's heart.

'The man's a liar,' he began to protest.

'Let the Lord settle that,' Hans bayed.

'Aye. Aye,' the crowd chorused, hoping for safety in numbers.

'Enough!' the captain shouted, and at once the mob fell silent. 'You two men will go before Count Boleslav. The rest of you will be taken to the castle.'

The soldier dug his spurs into his horse and rode through the crowd, giving orders to the rest of his troop. Soon a motley procession, headed by Petr and Hans, was making its way across the snow, closely guarded by the horsemen.

Unnoticed by the others, Josef left his hiding place and stood at the open door. He tried to think what to do for the best. Then, recalling the help Petr had given him when

Stephan was in danger, he strode after the others determined to speak up for his friend.

It was easy enough for him to join the stragglers crossing the bridge over the frozen river and, from then on, he was herded with the rest up the slippery track to the castle and into the courtyard.

13

'**W**ell, look who's here,' a familiar, rasping voice shouted.

Josef could hardly bring himself to turn round, knowing that he would be confronted by the blacksmith.

'What brings you here?' the man demanded.

'That's my business,' Josef growled.

The blacksmith laughed and pointed to a solitary figure in the far corner.

'If you're looking for your friend,' he said sarcastically, 'he's over there.' And with that, he swaggered away to a group of peasants who greeted him with laughter and slaps on the back.

Cursing under his breath, the woodman angrily pushed his way towards the miller who was standing with his back to the crowd, lost in thought. When he saw Josef standing before him, he smiled anxiously.

'You shouldn't have come,' he said.

'I couldn't stand by and do nothing,' Josef said. 'What's going on?'

'We're waiting to hear if Count Boleslav will hear the case.'

'No. I mean, what was that business at the mill all about?'

'I don't know,' Petr had to admit.

'Have you heard what they're saying about you?'

'Not so loud, my friend.'

'But it's all lies.'

'They're hungry.'

'Fools more like. Well, I'll speak up for you. You can be sure of that.'

Petr shook his head. 'Josef,' he said patiently, 'we've fought many battles together, but this is one I must fight alone. If you really want to help me, go to my wife. Tell her what has happened. Tell her especially not to worry.' He smiled. 'Cheer up. All is not lost. Count Boleslav is a greedy man but not a fool. He knows I would never dare cheat him of a single grain of his flour. Now go. There is nothing you can do here. Look after my wife — and be careful.'

With great reluctance, Josef nodded. He briefly clasped Petr's hand, and was gone. Petr watched the stooping figure thread its way through the crowd. He held his breath as it approached the gate and, as it slipped out unchallenged, he breathed easily again. He returned once more to thinking what he would say in his defence if Count Boleslav decided to hear the case.

Inside the great hall, silence reigned. The assembled company waited like statues while the Lord of Bletz sipped a goblet of wine. No one could have guessed from his demeanour that he was surprised, even shocked, by the charge levelled against the miller. It was, to his mind, out of character. Over the years, he had had many arguments with the man and had often wished to get rid of him. But dishonesty was not one of the man's failings, quite the reverse. He had been infuriated above all by the man's stubborn honesty. So what was it all about?

The noise of the rabble outside was beginning to get on the nerves of the commander of the garrison.

'What does your Lordship intend to do?' he dared to ask.

'*Do?*' His master's voice was deadly sharp.

'I must instruct the garrison, my Lord.'

'Of course you must. But not before I tell you.'

The battle-scarred face flushed and withdrew into silence. All eyes returned to Count Boleslav who took another sip of wine before addressing the priest seated at the end of the table.

'Well priest, what has Holy Writ to say about this?'

'Very little, my Lord,' Father Vilem replied, with an affability that suggested he was not going to be as easily rattled as the soldier.

The gathering waited for another angry rebuke but, instead, to their surprise the Count laughed.

'Come now, you can do better than that.' The voice was light, even playful, but there was no mistaking the authority of its demand.

Father Vilem hesitated. He knew exactly who was behind the demonstration — and why. He also knew that the blacksmith could not be trusted to keep the oaths sworn on the Bible, and that the man would not hesitate to resurrect the uncomfortable business of the cripple if the charge went against him. Under the circumstances, there seemed to be only one course of action.

'My Lord,' he said with his blandest smile, 'it is of course for you to judge the merits of the case against the miller — if you decide to hear it. But, since you have honoured me by asking for my opinion, I will say this. In my view, the miller has shown himself to be wilful, argumentative and, at times, disrespectful to your rank and position.'

The faint smile on his master's lips encouraged him to elaborate.

'Your Lordship has been most patient with the man, no doubt out of consideration for the poor souls who elected him headman. But the question I've been asking myself is, would those same peasants elect him today?'

Father Vilem paused to give Count Boleslav a chance to speak. But the only response was raised eyebrows that invited him to go on. He now chose his words carefully.

'I must confess,' he said with an unpleasant dryness in his mouth, 'that for some time I've been unhappy at so much responsibility being in such untutored hands. Perhaps, my Lord, the time has come to depart from tradition and to choose the headman yourself.'

Count Boleslav's hooded eyes closed for a moment, and a ripple of movement disturbed the listening statues.

'If this is your wish,' the priest was saying, 'you may be sure of the full blessing of the church. As for the peasants, having placed themselves outside the law, I doubt if they would even notice the loss of a minor privilege in return for being allowed to go unpunished.'

The priest's speech was greeted with silence all round. Many wondered why he had made it. Was it ambition for more power than he had already? Or was it simply greed for a high place at the Lord's table in the forthcoming feasts?

Father Vilem sat with bowed head, trying to maintain an outward show of confidence he did not feel. The meeting with the blacksmith had made it necessary to damn the miller. But did it coincide with the longings of his master? Try as he would, he could not stop the beads of perspiration forming in the folds of fat on his face and neck, or the trembling in his podgy fingers clasped on his enormous belly.

Meanwhile, Count Boleslav was staring into space, lightly running an index finger round the lip of the goblet. Suddenly he gave a loud guffaw, rose from his seat and strode to the priest, heartily thumping him on the back. For once, years of self-control vanished as Father Vilem smiled with unashamed relief and mopped the sweat from his brow with the sleeve of his habit.

'You read my mind to perfection,' the Count declared gaily, drawing applause from the gathering who wished to convey that they had had exactly the same idea. 'Bring them in,' the Count instructed the commander. 'But keep them well back. I can't bear their stinking breath.'

Calling to Father Vilem to sit beside him, the Lord of Bletz settled into his chair, holding out his goblet for more wine.

Events now moved swiftly. The trial, as Petr soon discovered, was no more than a hollow mockery of justice. At the outset, Count Boleslav warned that everyone who had taken part in the demonstration would be punished unless it was proved that they had been justly provoked. He then proceeded to listen only to Hans, who claimed to have seen the miller put a sack of grain to one side while he was repairing a chain at the mill; and to Vislav who said he had also witnessed the deed. Petr was given no opportunity to defend himself, all his protestations were overruled. The priest testified that the accusers were God-fearing, loyal peasants, leaving the outcome of the trial in no doubt. All that remained was for the Count to pass sentence.

'You have been found guilty of the crime of which you stand accused,' he told the bewildered miller. 'This crime was committed not only against me, but against your fellow peasants who trusted you. For this, the sentence I pass on you is banishment from Bletz for the remainder of your natural life.'

Banishment. The word brought a gasp of horror from the peasants crowded together at the back of the hall. Petr, shocked and pale, swayed under its impact.

The Count's words seemed to be coming from a great distance. 'You have until dawn tomorrow to be out of Bletz. If you ever return your punishment will be death by hanging...'

The severity of the sentence seemed never-ending.

'... I charge the rest of you to see that this sentence is carried out, using any means necessary...'

But why? Why? The question kept repeating itself in Petr's tortured mind. Why had Count Boleslav accepted the blacksmith's lies as the truth? Why had he refused to allow him, Petr, to speak?

'... The rest of you will be allowed to go... There will be no more elections for headman. You have shown yourselves incapable of choosing wisely. In future, I will choose the headman myself.'

And suddenly Petr understood the true meaning of the trial. It had been used as an excuse to remove one of their most important rights. He could have wept for the peasants who were now at the full mercy of their Lord.

'I shall announce the new headman at the Feast of Christmas.'

'God bless the Lord of Bletz,' the priest boomed.

'God bless the Lord of Bletz,' the peasants echoed, thinking only of their escape from flogging.

No one seemed to give a thought for the poor man condemned, who stood with head defiantly erect and fists clenched at his side. No one except the blacksmith, who tried to catch the priest's eye and, failing, turned instead to his pock-marked henchman and slapped him on the back.

The men of Bletz came early, while it was still dark, with feet quietly crunching on the packed snow. Many of them carried sticks, though few expected to need them. It was just good to have something firm and straight to hold on to.

When the party reached Petr's dwelling, it silently formed itself into a half-circle facing the door. In the glimmer of candlelight escaping through cracks in the walls, it was possible to see the strain on the men's faces. They could hear the couple moving about inside; they heard the woman's sobs and the man's low, gruff voice trying to console her. With the passion and anger of the day before gone, they felt confused and ashamed at what they had done.

As the sky slowly lightened, the men looked uneasily at their new leader who stood immediately opposite the door. Suddenly the light inside was extinguished and a few moments later, the door opened to reveal the miller and his wife. Their bodies were bent under the weight of the bundles they carried on their backs.

Seeing the men, the woman gave a cry and her husband put his arm round her to comfort her. Holding on to each other, they slowly walked through the ring of onlookers. From force of habit, a man ran forward to close the door they had left ajar. It was a pathetic and unnecessary gesture, but it expressed the way many of them felt.

Not a single word was spoken as the couple trudged through the village, followed at a respectful distance by the others. At the village boundary, as though by some unspoken agreement, the men drew to a halt, leaving Petr and his wife to struggle on together through the snow.

A bellow of triumph exploded in the stillness of the grey dawn.

'He's gone for good, my friends,' Hans shouted, unable to contain himself any longer and waving his stick in the air.

'We're well rid of him,' Vislav laughed. 'Three cheers for Hans,' he called.

The response was less than half-hearted and it made the blacksmith scowl. Even in banishment Petr seemed to rob him of being able to savour his triumph to the full. He turned furiously on his heel and stalked back towards the village, followed by Vislav and Lobvic.

'Let's go home,' a voice muttered and, with one accord, the men threw down their sticks and slowly walked away.

14

For the child living in the mountains, Christmas Day began like any other — at dawn, with a freezing mist swirling round the snow-covered ledge. The eagle, as was its habit, soon flew off in search of prey, leaving the boy to breakfast in solitude on the provisions collected each week from the cave. With a blanket over his shoulders, Stephan happily settled to the food which he still preferred to the eagle's diet. It was one of many inconsistencies in a strange existence that was changing him, quite rapidly, into an uncanny mixture of half boy, half bird of prey.

In bodily form he was still a crippled child. But the sounds he now made mimicked the language of the bird, and the haughty expression on his face mirrored the eagle's imperial countenance. Like the bird, he hopped from foot to foot when something puzzled him or made him unsure and, with eagle-like movements, he shook his mop of fair hair when he was angry. Gone, completely it seemed, was the frightened creature who had been abducted from its innocent life with the hare.

Even more fundamental than these outward signs, a new Stephan was emerging with a fierce, unpredictable nature that helped him face the rigours and dangers of his wild life with growing confidence and independence. If only he could have flown, the illusion would have been complete. There was a part of him which knew that this inability to fly marked him as a creature who was essentially different from the eagle, but flying every day with the bird imbued him with such feelings of mastery and power that he was tricked into believing his strength matched that of his mighty guardian.

Christmas morning had barely got underway when his real strength — not his imaginary strength — was severely tested. He was sighted by two marauding sparrow hawks who, sensing his defencelessness, began to attack him with repeated dives aimed at dislodging him from his narrow perch.

For a while he successfully warded them off by screeching and waving his arms. Then, as they persisted, he grabbed a blanket and flapped it like a pair of huge wings. But the attacks kept coming and gradually the effort of dealing with them began to exhaust him. For the first time, he felt afraid and he searched the sky, hoping to see the eagle coming to his aid. Overhead the hawks hovered, preparing for their next assault.

It came, as ever, without warning as one of them dived with beak open and talons ready to claw at his face. He shrieked and frantically waved the blanket until the bird swooped away below the level of the ledge. Before he had time to recover, the second bird was diving at him and, in the flurry, it caught the blanket in its claws and jerked him across the ledge. Another second and he would have toppled over, but some presence of mind made him let the blanket go and he was sent reeling backwards against the cliff.

For a moment, he was left dazed and defenceless. Then, above the raucous cries of the hawks who scented victory, there was a noise which made the boy's heart leap. It was the high-pitched whine of a body hurtling through the air.

The two marauders vainly tried to escape the thunderbolt from the sky. One bird was immediately seized by deadly talons and, with a spine-chilling shriek, the eagle snapped its back. The other, making a frenzied bid to escape, dropped the blanket which fell a few feet and then opened in a huge fluttering shape. But its end was as swift as that of its companion and it fell in a lifeless confusion of feathers after the blanket, which was gently floating down towards the rocks.

Stephan watched the swift dispatch of his assailants with the appraising eyes of one predator observing another make a kill. No longer in danger, he too gave a triumphant screech and the eagle, calmly circling back to the ledge, responded with a satisfied squawk. Proudly, the boy extended his neck and held his head high.

From its usual perch, the bird regarded him with silent approval. Then, like a teacher who decides to give his pupil an unexpected reward, it put its head on one side and uttered an inviting croak. Recognizing the call, the boy immediately scrambled across the ledge and dangled his feet over the edge. The bird hopped on to his shoulders and lifted him out into space.

They had flown together so often now that Stephan had learned the feel of the different movements in the air and, sensing an up-current, he waited for the moment when the eagle would carry them skywards. Almost immediately, the great wings began to move in slow, measured beats and they soared steadily upwards.

After climbing for a while, Stephan prepared for the flight to level out. But to his surprise the climb went on. He squawked questioningly, but the eagle made no reply. They were travelling through dense cloud and it was impossible to know where they were going — except upwards. Relent-lessly, the wings kept up their steady rhythm until the cloud began to thin and, suddenly, they were in a world of radiantly clear sunlight.

Stephan gasped in wonder at a range of mountain peaks, higher than any he had seen before. Below him the tops of the clouds hung like a giant bed of goose feathers. And still they climbed until they were level with the highest peaks. For the first time the eagle spoke. A peremptory squawk announced the end of their ascent and, with its wings outstretched, it glided round in a wide, graceful arc.

A thousand feet above the clouds, with no other living creatures in sight, with only space — so much space — around him, Stephan wanted the flight to go on and on.

Over there! he screeched, pointing to the other side of the mountains.

That's not my territory, the bird squawked.

It is. Take it!

The challenge was irresistible. With a shriek, the eagle circled back, casually flicked a wing and dived towards a flat ridge between two peaks. It flew low over the ridge, then glided serenely out into space. Another shriek announced its arrival in new territory.

Dive! the boy urged and obediently the bird rolled over and plummeted down towards the clouds.

Soon they were plunging through thick mist again and the pattern of their descent changed to steep racing glides, veering first one way and then another, flying so fast that Stephan feared they would crash against some hidden cliff. But with uncanny skill, the eagle seemed able to sense danger before it was visible and at last they emerged safely beneath the clouds.

They flew over a huge river of ice, racing along its entire length to a torrent of water gushing from a dark cavern at the glacier's end. And then on to a distant pine forest.

Skimming the tree tops, Stephan kicked at the branches, sending flocks of small birds flying from their perches with fearful cries and forest animals running to safety.

In the end, the sight of all this tempting food was too much for the eagle. With a squawk, it abruptly dived into a clearing and deposited Stephan in the snow.

Stay there! it ordered and immediately flew off, unmoved by the furious shrieks from the boy.

Snorting with frustration, Stephan scrambled to his feet, brushing the snow from his arms and body. He grabbed a handful of snow and hurled it at a nearby tree. Standing knee deep in snow he looked moodily at his new surroundings.

In all directions, he could see nothing but the close pattern of straight tree trunks. Nothing moved. The forest was perfectly silent. Suddenly a noise which he did not recognize made him stiffen.

'Hodie Christus natus est.

Hodie salvator apparuit,' a querulous voice was singing.

Stephan stared in its direction, but the owner of the voice could not be seen. He put his head on one side, shifting his weight from one foot to the other.

'Hodie in terra canunt angeli,' the voice sang, getting closer. It sent Stephan hobbling away to hide behind a tree.

'Hodie exultant justi dicentes.

Gloria in —'

The singing abruptly stopped and Stephan cautiously peered round the tree. A short distance from him was a strange, dark creature that seemed to be very interested in the prints left by him and the eagle in the snow. Stephan froze out of sight behind the tree.

On the edge of the clearing, an old man shook his head at the curious marks in the snow. Wisps of white hair protruded beneath the hood of an ancient black cloak and hanging down his chest, like a scarf, was a long white beard. The hem of his cloak and the brown robe he wore beneath it were sodden from trailing in the snow. In his arms, he carried a bundle of twigs.

He whistled between cracked teeth and as he frowned, the paper-thin skin on his face creased in a fine network of lines. He turned pale eyes to the sky, and sighed. Returning to the marks in the snow, his eyes followed the trail of uneven footprints. He crossed himself and in slow, faltering steps walked towards the tree behind which Stephan was hiding. The shock of finding a small boy flattened against the tree like a cornered animal made him drop the twigs in surprise.

'A child,' he gasped. 'A boy!'

He listened open-mouthed to the low hissing noises Stephan made to warn him off.

'Who are you?' the old man asked, finding his voice at last.

He took a step closer only to be stopped by an ear-piercing shriek. He fumbled under his cloak for the crucifix hanging round his neck, and listened in horror to the harsh, rasping noises coming from the boy's throat.

'Dear Lord in Heaven,' he murmured, 'what have we here?'

As though in answer, the boy uttered another shriek which sent the old man falling to his knees.

'Merciful Lord, protect me,' he prayed with trembling hands clasped together. He looked at the boy and again asked, 'Who are you?'

His question was greeted with threatening croaks and an impenetrable stare.

'Tell me child, who are you?' he asked once more. 'What is your name?'

The loud screech which followed made the old man flinch. Then, abruptly, the boy arrogantly tossed his head and proceeded to parade round him in a circle. The sight of the child's ungainly limp drew a compassionate exclamation from the kneeling figure who cried, 'You're a cripple!' and started to get up, only to be sent immediately to his knees again by another screech from the boy who had interpreted this as a sign of attack.

'You look like a boy,' the frightened old man said under his breath, 'you walk like a cripple. But you sound like some great bird.'

For several moments, neither of them moved or spoke. Then, plucking up enough courage to try again, the old man very cautiously struggled to his feet, holding out his arms with palms turned to the boy to show that he meant no harm.

Stephan croaked warily, watching this with the utmost suspicion.

Encouraged, the old man took a step forward, saying in a tremulous voice, 'Don't be afraid. I'm not going to hurt you.'

The quiet, gentle voice and the complete absence of threatening signals greatly confused Stephan. He was used to creatures which either fled from him, or attacked him. Shifting his weight from foot to foot, he allowed the creature to come closer. But when it touched his face, he shrieked with such force that it went reeling backwards into the snow.

The old man clasped his hands again in a silent prayer and then bravely tried again.

Very slowly, one tentative movement at a time, he stood up and approached the boy, expecting at any moment to be met with another bird-like outburst. But none came, not even when, with the greatest caution, he reached out and placed trembling fingertips on the boy's head.

Without warning, the boy reached up, grabbed his wrist and yanked it down. He was holding it so tightly that the old man winced with pain but did not dare cry out or move in case it disturbed the boy who was looking at the back of his hand, as though he had never seen such a thing before. Then the boy turned it over and examined the palm, scraping dirty fingers across it so that broken fingernails dug into the frail skin. Mercifully, the boy abruptly let his wrist go, but took to prodding the old man's face and even pulling his beard. Throughout this odd, painful ritual, the old man managed to preserve a shaky smile till, with a brief squawk, the boy seemed to indicate that he was satisfied.

The old man gratefully rubbed his wrist, and sighed. He was surprised to see the child do the same. He sighed again, and once more the boy copied him. Soon, it developed into a game in which they took turns to take a deep breath and blow it out in the other's face.

'Who are you, child?' the old man asked when the boy had tired of the game. 'Where do you come from?'

The boy cawed uncomprehendingly, scooped a handful of snow and threw it in the air. He waited expectantly for the old man to do the same.

'My name is Bartholomew,' the old man said. 'Bartholomew.'

The boy hopped impatiently from foot to foot.

'Bartholomew,' the old man repeated, pointing at his chest. 'Bar-thol-o-mew.'

The boy, who had been watching carefully, opened his mouth but only succeeded in producing a meaningless grunt.

'Bar-thol-o-mew,' the old man reiterated.

Once more, the boy opened his mouth and this time, after several false starts and much encouragement, he at last managed, 'Ba. . . Ba. . .'

If Bartholomew had known that these were the first near-human sounds uttered by Stephan for a long time, his delight would have been very great indeed.

'I live over there,' he said, 'in a hut.'

'Ba. . . Ba. . . ,' Stephan intoned with a deeply serious frown.

'Come with me and I'll show you.'

Smiling, the old man held out his hand and then, sensing the boy wasn't going to take it, he started to walk away, beckoning to him to follow.

It was an odd little procession that hesitantly made its way from the clearing. In the lead was a frail old man who talked in a quiet, reassuring voice, followed by a silent boy in ragged, filthy clothes whose bearing was proud in spite of the awkward swaying of his small body.

They had not gone very far when Bartholomew stopped and pointed through the trees.

'There it is,' he said. 'That's my hut.'

Stephan frowned at the small wooden builing with smoke rising from a hole in the roof. The smell of wood smoke made his nose twitch and he backed away.

'Don't be afraid,' Bartholomew said with a smile. 'Come.'

The boy seemed reassured by this and they were about to move on when a distant screech brought a sudden and dramatic change in his behaviour. He emitted a shrill, jubilant shriek and immediately he was leaping through the snow as fast as his limp would allow, back to the clearing.

Bartholomew called after him, beseeching him to stop. But

his cries went unheeded and, gathering up his long garments, he ran in pursuit.

As Stephan entered the clearing, he gave a loud screech which was answered almost immediately by a familiar shriek. In the next moment, the eagle dived into view and landed beside him with its usual cool assurance.

Bartholomew reached the edge of the clearing in time to see the boy and the huge bird squawking angrily at each other. He stared in wide-eyed amazement as the boy knelt in the snow and the bird hopped on to his shoulders. In disbelief, his hand went to his crucifix as the bird flapped its wings and lifted the boy into the air. Then, realizing that the pair would soon be gone, he ran into the clearing waving his arms and calling, 'Come back. Come back.'

From above the tree tops Stephan looked down on the diminishing figure waving to him.

'Ba. . . Ba. . . Ba. . . Oo,' he shouted, waving back.

'Bar-thol-o-mew,' the reedy voice cried, barely audible above the thrashing wings.

Keep still, the eagle squawked with its mind on the long flight ahead.

Bartholomew stood in the clearing gazing at the sky long after the eagle and the boy had gone. In all his many years as a hermit in the forest, meditating and studying, he had never encountered such a mystery. How had a crippled boy come to talk like a bird — and such a bird? A bird that could lift the boy without effort to the sky? And yet, the boy *was* a boy. He could still feel that firm grip on his wrist; still picture the frown on the boy's face as he tried to say his name.

Unable to answer any of these questions, Bartholomew slowly walked back to his hut, resolved to keep daily watch in case the boy should ever return.

15

In the fading light of Christmas afternoon, the woodman knelt in front of the fire, patiently blowing the smouldering logs into some semblance of life. His outer garments and leggings were still covered with snow, as were Marta's. She sat shivering on a stool beside him, huddled into herself to get warm.

They had attended morning Mass and then, taking all the provisions they could spare, had gone into the forest to look for the miller and his wife. It was not easy to find them but, after searching for several hours, they had spotted a tell-tale trail of smoke and, sure enough, it led them to the deep glade where the couple were now living. They were greeted with a mixture of joy and alarm by the exiles, who seemed to be in reasonable health, but exhausted by the cold and the daily struggle for survival in such harsh conditions.

The four of them had spent what was left of the daylight working and talking together. The two women prepared a simple meal and the men laboured on the rough shelter erected by the miller, strengthening the walls and roof timbers with tree trunks which the woodman felled and split.

'I'm glad we went,' Marta said, cheered by the sight of flames beginning to lick round the logs.

Josef smiled and nodded. 'I'll go again — soon,' he said, giving the fire a last blow.

Marta looked anxiously at him.

'They'll need help,' he shrugged, 'to live through winter.'

He sat back on his haunches, satisfied that the fire could now look after itself. Still on his knees, he held out a hand to Marta.

'Say a prayer for us,' he said, 'for our dear friends — and our boy in the mountains.'

Christmas night was celebrated in the castle of Bletz in a blaze of light. The great hall glowed with a multitude of candles while Count Boleslav and his favoured guests feasted on an endless succession of dishes — wild boar, venison and game birds of every description. The faces round the long table were flushed with the wine that flowed like water and the heat of the huge logs blazing in the open hearth.

Outside burning torches and braziers, blown in the wind, filled the courtyard with flickering yellow flames. In time-honoured custom, peasants and soldiers alike sat down together at trestle-tables, all hostility forgotten, as the poor guests of their Lord.

They gorged themselves on salt pork and oat cakes — food such as they had not seen for many months — and drank ale from the castle brewery. The noise of so many voices, shouting and laughing and singing, could have been heard from miles away. Many were sick from over-indulging stomachs that were not used to so much food; others were sick with the ale. Everyone was drunk and no one would have wanted it otherwise, for this was Christmas night, a night when the cares and hardships of life were to be eaten and drunk into oblivion. And, in the midst of this orgy, the blacksmith sat roaring with delight as his faithful cronies kept raising their mugs and toasting him as the next headman of Bletz.

At the height of the festivities a fanfare of horns announced the imminent arrival of Count Boleslav. As a body, the crowd struggled to its feet, many had to be helped or supported. Sweating faces and eyes fogged with drink turned to the door through which the Lord of Bletz and his entourage made their entrance. Those who were close enough, or just sober enough to see, gasped at the magnificence of his robes and jewels.

The commander of the garrison banged with the flat of his sword on a table. 'Silence for the Lord of Bletz,' he bawled. The crowd, swaying on its feet, fell into a stupefied silence.

'Peasants of Bletz, I do not intend to interrupt your

celebrations for long,' Count Boleslav began, to a rowdy cheer from the crowd. 'But today is the day I promised to name the man I have chosen to be your headman —'

There was a loud crash as a peasant, too drunk to stand up any longer, fell across one of the tables, sending mugs and food flying in all directions. The burly commander would have sent soldiers to haul the man away but the indulgent smile on his master's thin lips stopped him.

The blacksmith, who could hardly contain himself, was glaring at the priest, willing him to turn in his direction.

'The man I have chosen is well known to you all,' he heard the Count saying, and still the bloated face remained obstinately averted. 'He has proved himself to be a natural leader among you.' By now, the blacksmith was holding his breath, consumed with murderous thoughts of what he would do if the priest had not honoured their pact. 'I declare your headman is the blacksmith of Bletz, known as Hans.'

The crowd went wild. Arms waved in the air. Frenzied shouts and cheering went echoing round the high walls.

The chosen man himself stood quite still, swaying slightly, head back, eyes gleaming and an idiotic grin spreading from ear to ear. He heard the voices of Vislav and Lobvic shouting their congratulations; he felt hands seize him and lift him up. In a cloud of triumph, he allowed himself to be carried shoulder high around the courtyard.

'It seems I have made a popular choice,' Count Boleslav laconically observed.

'As ever, my Lord, you have shown great wisdom throughout this affair,' Father Vilem replied, well satisfied.

With masterly skill, he had manipulated the Lord's choice by comparing the drawbacks of choosing an honest man, who might prove to be as stubborn as the miller, with the advantages of selecting a man whose greed would make him an unresisting mouthpiece for the Lord's commands.

'A bully and a rogue,' he had said, 'is not to be trusted. But such a man can always be bought with a sack of grain.' And thinking ahead to the night of the announcement, he had added, 'And so too can the other peasants — if they are given plenty to eat and drink at the Christmas feast.'

The Lord of Bletz had not only taken his advice, he had sat him on his right hand at the high table in the great hall. Surveying the riot going on in front of him, Father Vilem had no doubts — the day had been a great personal triumph.

Part Two

From forest to castle

16

'Mm . . . I love the spring!' Bartholomew declared, filling his old lungs with a deep breath of air.

'Huh?'

'Spring, my boy — *spring*!' The hermit opened his arms and took another deep breath, beaming at the sky. 'Everything you see around you is — spring.'

Stephan looked at him with a stern frown.

'Forgive me,' Bartholomew smiled. 'Let me explain.' He spoke slowly and deliberately, emphasizing words with gestures to make their meaning clear. 'We call this time of year — spring. In spring the sun shines. The snow melts — disappears. Everything that seemed dead comes alive again — reborn. The forest is full of animals. Birds make nests in the trees. Flowers grow —' He stooped to pick a bloom from a carpet of white anemones. 'Look. This is a flower. We call this one the wind-flower.' He passed the delicate, star-shaped bloom to Stephan who held it in cupped hands and regarded it with great concentration. Then, he looked up and in a rather grand way surveyed the scene before them.

'Sprr . . . ingg,' he announced after a struggle.

Nearly three years had passed since their first meeting and in the interval he had grown considerably. He was now almost as tall as the old man, who had shrunk a little, and his fair hair cascaded down his back. He was dressed in a bizarre assortment of clothes — some of them left in the cave, others passed on to him by Bartholomew who had also given him the small wooden crucifix that hung by a string round his neck.

They walked leisurely through the pine trees, lit by beams of slanting sunlight, filtering through the dampness rising from the ground. Stephan's limp was as ungainly as ever, but his up-tilted head and solemn face gave him a striking appearance of poise.

Stephan rarely smiled, not because he was displeased or unhappy but because his natural bearing was proud and aloof. He listened attentively to Bartholomew, staring at him with a disconcerting penetration in his eyes.

After their first meeting, Bartholomew had kept his vow and had gone each day to the clearing to wait for the reappearance of the eagle and the strange child. But the weeks had gone by and he had begun to give up hope of ever seeing them again. Then early one morning, the noise of beating wings had brought him running from his hut and, to his great joy, he had seen the eagle swooping through the trees with the boy hanging beneath it.

Once landed, the bird had placed itself between the old man and the boy, squawking and flapping its wings to keep them apart. Then, for some reason known only to itself, it had relented and with a final screech had flown away. At once, the boy had come hobbling forward, eagerly shouting, 'Ba . . . Ba . . . Ba . . . Oo .'

That visit was the first of many. They were always at long and irregular intervals, and they always followed the same pattern. After making a great deal of fuss about leaving the boy, the eagle flew off and during its absence, the others walked in the forest or sat in the hut until it returned, demanding with impatient screeches to be gone.

Bartholomew used these visits to instruct the boy in the rudiments of human speech. At first, his pupil's progress was painfully slow and full of disappointments but gradually the boy learned to move his lips and tongue correctly to form words.

Improvements in speech brought more understanding and Bartholomew patiently sought to unravel some of the mysteries surrounding the boy. To his sorrow, he did not get very far, for the boy seemed not to know or to be unable to remember anything about his past — even his name. So, the hermit christened him Jan, after the beloved disciple.

'Now, Jan,' the hermit said, continuing with the lesson, 'after spring comes summer — *sum-mer*.'

'Sum-mer,' the boy repeated in his loud, flat voice.

'Good! In summer it is hot — fuff!' Bartholomew comically wiped his face with the end of his long white beard, drawing a rare smile from the boy.

'Fly!' Stephan said, pointing to the sky. 'Fly!'

'Yes, you can fly.'

'Fly!' the boy said with greater emphasis, trying to express a difficult thought. 'Sum-mer fly!'

'Yes. In summer you can fly.'

Stephan shook his head with frustration and gave a loud squawk, pointing at the sun.

'The sun? Is that what you mean? In summer you can fly to the sun?'

The boy vigorously nodded. 'Sun!' he said with a proud toss of his head.

'I think, Jan, you're trying to tell me that in summer the eagle carries you high in the sky — so high it feels you are flying to the sun. Is that correct?'

Stephan solemnly nodded.

'It must be wonderful to fly,' Bartholomew sighed. 'I can only tell you what happens on the earth. But that is wonderful too. Let me tell you what happens in autumn — au-tumn.'

'Orr-tum. Orr-tum,' Stephan repeated, rolling the r's in the back of his throat.

'Autumn, Jan, is very beautiful. And it is a sad time too. The leaves turn the colours of my fire — red and yellow and purple. Then they die and fall from the trees.' Bartholomew bent down and picked up a decaying hazel nut. 'In autumn I pick nuts like this one and berries that are good to eat.'

'Eat nuts,' Stephan said, pointing to his mouth.

'You eat nuts?'

'Mm.'

The hermit smiled. He had feared the boy shared the eagle's

prey and was relieved to learn that sometimes at least there was other food to eat. In fact, Stephan still lived on the provisions his father continued to leave each week in the cave.

'Now, after autumn comes winter. *Win-ter.*'

'Win-terr.'

'Very good. In winter the wind blows—oo! The snow falls — brrh!'

Bartholomew drew his cloak round him and shivered.

'Win-terr cold,' Stephan announced with slow thoughtfulness.

'Eagle —' He held out an arm to show how the bird covered him with its wing.

'In winter the eagle keeps you warm?'

'Worrmm.'

'In winter the fire keeps me warm. You like my fire, don't you? You can put logs on it when we get to the hut.'

The boy gave a friendly squawk.

'That's settled then!'

And in a happy, companionable mood they walked together towards the hermit's small dwelling.

It stood on a small grassy knoll in surroundings which, on that spring day, looked idyllic — encircled by trees with a stream running near by. In front of it, a small family of goats were tethered, while the hut itself was built of roughly hewn timbers with a thatched roof and low eaves which served as a shelter for piles of logs.

Inside, it was very small, dark and bare. The floor was trodden earth and the only furniture was a single table and stool, a straw mattress and a box in which Bartholomew kept his most treasured possession. The sole decoration in the room was a brass crucifix nailed to the wall above the bed. In the centre was an open fire which burned continuously throughout the year and above it an opening in the roof to let out the smoke. Everything in the room smelt of woodsmoke and, on the days when the wind blew the smoke back into the room, it made the atmosphere so thick that Bartholomew coughed continuously with watering eyes.

After an initial wariness, Stephan had come to enjoy the warmth of the fire and the sweet smell of burning pine logs. It was one of the things he looked forward to as he sat on the exposed mountain ledge thinking about his next visit to Bartholomew. But, like the hermit, he had no idea when it would be. It always happened without warning when the eagle, responding to some private urge, decided to make the long flight over the mountains. Why it continued to do so remained a mystery. Perhaps it needed to restate its supremacy over newly claimed territory; perhaps, it needed to prove to itself that it was still strong enough to carry the growing boy over such a long distance.

Stephan accepted the unpredictable timing of these visits with the same stoicism that he had learned to accept all aspects of his life with the eagle. He enjoyed the hours spent with the hermit receiving his patient instruction, but nothing compared with the freedom of flying with the bird whose majestic strength made it, in Stephan's mind, the undisputed master of all other creatures — including Bartholomew.

Returning from the walk, they came into the hut and took their customary places in front of the fire — Bartholomew perched on a stool, Stephan sitting cross-legged on the floor. They talked in a desultory way expecting at any moment to hear the sounds of the eagle's return. But as time passed and there was still no sign of the bird, Stephan began to grow restless. He got up and wandered round the room. Bartholomew watched him in silence. Then the boy opened the door and looked up at the sky.

'It'll come soon,' the old man said, trying to sound reassuring. 'Come and sit by the fire.'

Stephan shook his head and limped a few paces from the door, frowning at the long shadows of the trees on the grass. A little later, as the sun disappeared behind a dark cloud, he gave an anxious screech. It made the goats bleat, but brought no reassuring call from the sky. He screeched again — and again. Each time louder and more desperate than before.

Bartholomew listened to these panic-stricken cries with a face lined with concern. From his seat by the fire he could see the boy through the open door and his heart ached for him. He got to his feet and went outside to offer comfort. But the moment he put a hand on Stephan's shoulder he was violently thrust aside and the boy was running off through the trees, shrieking at the top of his voice.

The hermit bit his lip, wanting to follow and yet unnerved by the boy's wild, untouchable behaviour. He remained indecisively by the hut, listening to the never-ending cries in the clearing until, as the light began to fade, they suddenly stopped. He listened for a moment to the silence, then a rustling of leaves which heralded a cool gust of wind made him shiver. Gathering his ancient robe round him he returned briefly to the hut and emerged with a cloak to take out to Stephan.

He found the boy sitting on the grass with a ground mist rising round him, mutely gazing at the sky.

'You'll get cold out here,' he said, gently putting the cloak round Stephan's shoulders.

The boy made no reply, gave no sign that he had even noticed Bartholomew's presence or the cloak.

'Listen to me, Jan,' the hermit tentatively said. 'Perhaps the eagle isn't coming back.'

There was an angry screech from Stephen whose eyes were still locked on the sky.

'Perhaps it wants you to stay here.'

The screech of fury that followed made Bartholomew reach for his crucifix.

'Please listen to me, Jan,' he begged in a trembling voice. 'It will soon be dark. The eagle is not coming back today.'

In a violent flurry of movement, the boy threw off the

cloak, leaped to his feet and hurled himself at the old man, waving his arms and wildly shrieking. Bartholomew retreated to the edge of the clearing which seemed to satisfy the boy for, after making one or two menacing hisses, he disdainfully turned away and sat down again, cross-legged, to resume his vigil of the sky.

The hermit gave a resigned sigh and in a quiet, anxious voice called, 'Come in when you want to.' Greatly troubled, he returned to the hut where he knelt down and prayed.

Far away on the other side of the mountains, the golden eagle was perched on its windswept eyrie, staring into the darkness with fierce, unblinking eyes. It stretched out a wing in a habitual gesture and, for a moment, was disconcerted at not finding a familiar figure nestling against its body. It squawked impatiently and looked round the ledge. Finding itself alone, it closed its wing and shook its golden crest. The look in its eyes was hard and unrelenting.

It had to be done. In one swift decisive movement the eagle had wheeled away from its flight back to the clearing and had soared into the sky — alone. Its pride could endure nothing else. The boy creature was growing — already he was a heavy burden. A day might dawn when his weight became greater than the bird's strength, and that would be intolerable. Yes, it had to be done.

I am undefeated! the eagle shrieked. And, as an afterthought, it screeched a terrible warning — Let no one harm the boy creature!

17

The days followed one another, and Stephan hardly left the clearing. When he did, it was to wander alone in the forest and then return shortly afterwards to resume his silent vigil. For hour after hour he sat cross-legged on the ground, bleakly staring at the sky.

From the edge of the clearing Bartholomew watched him with growing anxiety. He saw the boy's normally bronzed face turn ashen grey from lack of food and, from time to time, he ventured closer with a bowl of gruel. But it was never touched. He begged Stephan to return to the hut, saying he could keep watch just as easily from there. But again there was no response. Nothing he said or did seemed to penetrate the wall of silence surrounding the boy who was locked in a private world from which he could only be released by a call from the sky.

Stephan's grief was beyond tears. It was a state of utter desolation in which his whole being ached for his old home on the perilous ledge with its open views across the mountains and the constant moaning of the wind. He longed to see that stern, imperious face again and to hear the harsh, authoritative voice. But more than anything, he desired with a desperate longing to be up in the sky once more with the air rippling past his face; to feel the blood rushing to his head as they swooped to the earth and the sudden lurch in his stomach as they soared to the clouds. Anything else was unthinkable.

But time is a great healer and, in time, it began to work its miracle on Stephan.

On the evening of the seventh day, Bartholomew came as usual to talk to him and, quite unexpectedly, the boy turned round to look at him. There was something in the boy's eyes — a look — which made the old man catch his breath. If he was not deceived, Bartholomew thought he detected a faint glimmer of recognition in the boy's expression.

'Jan?' he asked, hardly daring to hope.

He held his breath and, after a moment, the boy gave a little nod. It was the merest movement of the head, but it was enough to transform the lines of worry on the old man's face into a welcoming smile of joy.

'Jan,' he breathed with tears of relief in his eyes.

Stephan frowned at him, trying to remember who he was. Then, drawing himself up, he said with unexpected firmness, 'Eagle —' And shook his head.

'Yes, Jan,' Bartholomew gravely said, 'the eagle has gone.'

He waited anxiously for Stephan to speak again or show some sign of grief. But the boy sat with a distant look in his eyes as though he was trying to remember something. Then he turned again to Bartholomew and declared in a quiet but determined voice, 'Fly. Want to fly.'

The old man knelt beside him.

'I know,' he said tenderly. 'But only the eagle can do that.'

'*Must* fly.'

'No, Jan. You cannot fly — only the eagle can do that. The eagle carried you. And one day it had to end — when you grew too heavy, or when the eagle grew too old.'

There was an angry squawk from Stephan.

'Look at my hands,' Bartholomew said. 'Once they were as strong as yours. Look at them now. They are wrinkled and frail. One day the eagle will be like my hands.'

The corners of the boy's mouth turned down in a disdainful expression as he studied the outstretched hands. He compared them with his own, looking repeatedly from one pair to the other until, at last, he nodded and gave such a pitiful sigh that the old man's heart went out to him.

'Don't be sad, Jan,' he said. 'You are stronger than the eagle.'

Stephan vehemently shook his head.

'Yes, you are. Not in the ways the eagle is strong, but in other ways. Come with me, Jan. Come, and I'll do my best to show you.'

With creaking limbs, Bartholomew got to his feet and offered a hand to Stephan. At first the boy refused it and then, finding he was too weak to get up unaided, he allowed the old man to help him up and with faltering steps he was supported back to the hut.

18

As soon as Stephan was fit enough, Bartholomew launched into the education of his pupil with great enthusiasm, though he soon found he was dealing with a wild, rebellious spirit who was not going to be tamed without a struggle. Simple, everyday matters such as trying to encourage Stephan to eat with a knife or spoon instead of always using his fingers provoked much argument. And when he suggested cutting Stephan's hair, he was met with such a barrage of squawking that he had to drop the whole idea. He failed also to persuade Stephan to sleep indoors on the mattress he had made from an old blanket stuffed with dried bracken and heather.

But in spite of all these ups and downs, Stephan gradually became accustomed to the domestic life of the hermit. Some tasks he positively enjoyed and could be allowed to do on his own, such as gathering wood and fetching water from the stream in an old goatskin bag. And he was fascinated by the snares Bartholomew set for catching hares and soon became more successful at it than the old man himself. He learned to milk the goats though, at first, he handled them so roughly that they were in danger of not giving any milk and Bartholomew would have barred him completely had the boy not protested so vigorously. As it was, they settled for a compromise in which Stephan would be allowed to milk the goats provided it was under Bartholomew's supervision.

Occasionally, the hermit was presented with an unexpected pleasure — the day, for example, when he found Stephan, without any prompting from himself, hard at work repairing the roof that had been damaged in a storm. With gratitude and delight he watched the boy gather materials and fill in the holes in the crude thatch — a task that would have sorely taxed Bartholomew's strength and agility. Indeed, he found himself relying more and more on the health and vigour of his companion in the hundred and one mundane tasks necessary for their survival.

From the outset Bartholomew tried to enlarge his pupil's knowledge beyond purely physical skills. He talked about the world and its mysteries; about the sun and the moon, taking Stephan outside on clear nights to show him the stars and their constellations. He was never quite sure how much his pupil understood, but it was an act of faith for him and he persisted.

Sometimes, he talked about God, whom Stephan pictured as a giant eagle flying above the clouds, and told him stories from the Bible. Stephan's favourites were nearly all from the Old Testament and concerned heroic battles — the fight between David and Goliath; Joshua at the walls of Jericho. These stories always prompted remarks about the eagle — how *it* would have slain Goliath, how *it* would have sent the walls of Jericho tumbling with one mighty shriek.

The old man was only too aware that the eagle was never far from the boy's mind. There were days when Stephan withdrew into himself and became unapproachable. Bartholomew learned from bitter experience that it was best not to interfere, but to endure the raucous bird-talk and leave him free to stomp off into the forest alone.

It was rare for Stephan not to return before nightfall and Bartholomew was usually waiting for him at the door. The sight of him limping back through the trees, often covered in mud, never failed to melt the old man's heart and to reassure the boy that all was forgiven, he would encourage him to open the box and take out his most precious possession.

This was a large leather-bound Bible. The handwritten Latin text was incomprehensible to Stephan but, from the very beginning, the small, brightly coloured paintings made a deep and lasting impression on him.

At first, Bartholomew refused to allow him to handle it, fearing that the boy's rough hands would damage the pages. And one day, while the old man was outside, Stephan was tempted to take it out for himself. When Bartholomew came in unexpectedly and found the boy sitting on the floor with the precious Bible lying on the earth, he flew into such a rage that Stephan was genuinely shocked and meekly allowed Bartholomew to put it back in its box. The incident remained a bone of contention between them for several weeks though, to make up for his disobedience, he finally agreed to sleep indoors and even have his hair cut.

Days, weeks, the seasons, followed each other in natural rotation and became years — years which saw great developments in Stephan. He would never be tall like his father, but his boyish figure developed into a compact, lithe body as he grew up, and his speech made such improvement that it was hard to imagine he had been unable to talk as a child.

But the years spent with the eagle had left an indelible mark. The flame that had been lit during that time — the flame that had transformed him from a frightened animal-child to a self-confident, wild boy — the flame that would always illuminate his personality in ways which marked him as strangely different from other people — this flame, for all the hermit's tutelage, stubbornly refused to go out.

By turns, Bartholomew loved Stephan for it and was exasperated by it. He could never forget the sight of the child flying with the eagle, or the boy's abject grief when the bird abandoned him. But he wished with all his heart that one day Stephan would be released from the eagle's influence.

19

They were out in the foothills of the mountains one day in late autumn gathering wortle-berries when Stephan suddenly asked, 'Did you write your Bible, Bartholomew?'

The hermit, who was lost in his own thoughts, looked up in surprise, grunted, and shook his head.

'But you can read it?' Stephan persisted in the gruff voice of a boy whose voice had recently broken.

'Oh yes.'

'Who taught you to read it?'

Bartholomew stopped picking berries for a moment and smiled to himself as he recalled a face from the distant past.

'A funny-looking man with a squint in one eye,' he said, screwing up his face and pointing a stained finger at his left eye. 'But he was a man of God — a priest. And a man of great patience.'

'Did he live in the hut?'

'Goodness no. I learned to read long before I came to live in the forest.'

This came as a great surprise to Stephan who had never imagined Bartholomew living anywhere but in the hut.

'Where did you live before?' he asked, intrigued.

The old man seemed reluctant to answer but, in the end, said, 'In a castle.'

'A castle!' Stephan's eyes lit up with excitement. 'Why?'

'Because I was born there,' Bartholomew replied briefly. 'Now, will you please get on with your picking or we'll never finish before nightfall.'

But Stephan's curiosity had been well and truly roused.

'Why were you born in a castle, Bartholomew? Why? Why?' The hectoring tone of his voice was one that the old man knew only too well and it meant there would be no peace until the question was properly answered. Sighing, he perched on a nearby rock which brought Stephan gleefully scrambling across to sit beside him.

'I was born in a castle, Jan, because it belonged to my father.'

'Was he a king?' the boy asked as he helped himself to a handful of berries from his basket.

'If you eat all the berries now, there'll be none to take back with us,' Bartholomew said sternly.

Stephan snorted and asked again, 'Was he a king?'

'Not exactly,' the old man replied, looking ruefully at the meagre gathering of berries left in Stephan's basket. 'He was a lord. But he was like a king to the people who lived in the castle and the villages round about. They did everything for him. They grew all the food he ate and cooked it for him. All he had to do was order them about.'

'I do not think I would like to be ordered about.'

'No. I'm sure you wouldn't. And neither did they. But they were only peasants and they belonged to my father. So they had to obey him.'

'Why?'

'Because they were afraid of him. And because they were afraid of the soldiers living in the castle.'

'The eagle was not afraid. I am not afraid. Were you afraid?'

'No. But not because I was brave, I hasten to add. It was simply because I was the Lord's son and I treated the peasants just like my father did. If my mother had been alive, things might have been different. But she died giving birth to me. So you see, Jan, I am like you — I never knew my mother. But at least I knew my father.'

'You are my father, Bartholomew.'

'Not your real father.'

'What was your real father like?'

'I didn't see much of him. He was always out hunting, or riding with his friends. I spent all my time with the soldiers.'

'They were cruel.'

'I didn't think so at the time. I thought they were magnificent. They carried swords and wore armour that flashed in the sun. I remember — it was one of the few times I spoke to my father — I remember begging him to let me be a soldier when I grew up. He roared with laughter and ordered one of them to teach me how to fight with a sword.'

'A sword! I want to fight with a sword.'

'I practised every day, hacking away at a sack stuffed with straw. My father was delighted and made me show off my skills to his friends. I was very proud of myself at the time. Now, it fills me with shame.'

'Why? Why are you not proud of yourself now?'

'If you'll be quiet for a moment, I'll tell you. One day the priest I was telling you about — the one with the funny eye — came to live in the castle. And one of his tasks was to teach me to read. My father couldn't read but for some reason — pride I expect — he wanted me to read. I have to admit, Jan, that I was a very bad pupil. I wanted to be outside practising with my sword and not stuck in a room with a priest. I made his life miserable. I called him all kinds of names which I blush to think of now. But he persisted. I suppose, poor man, he had to because he had been ordered to by my father. Anyway, he persisted and, almost against my will, I learned to read. And that, dear Jan, was the beginning of the end.'

'Beginning — end? I don't understand.'

'Patience. Let me explain. The priest taught me to read the Bible — as I would like to teach you one day — and when I read about the ministry of our Lord Jesu I was very confused. He was a king — the greatest the world has ever known — but he didn't live in a castle with servants and soldiers. He was as poor as the peasants living in the huts around the castle. When I asked the priest about this, he refused to answer. I think he was too frightened. So I asked my father and it made him very angry. He called for the priest and sent him away. And he ordered me to read no more books. But I disobeyed him. Yes, Jan, I disobeyed my father and went on reading — secretly. And the more I read, the more confused I became. You asked me what my father was like. Well, I'll tell you. He was greedy, selfish, and cruel.'

'Your father was a bad man, Bartholomew. But you are not bad. You are good.'

'I did something that was very wrong.'

'What was that?'

Bartholomew gave a deep sigh and a sad, faraway look came into his old eyes.

'One day, quite unexpectedly, my father died. And I became Lord in his place.'

'You? A lord?'

'Yes.'

'What was it like?'

'Very confusing. I didn't know what to do. I wasn't much older than you are now and my father's old friends who still lived in the castle kept telling me to do this thing and that thing until my head was spinning. Then, early one morning — I can remember it now after all these years — the sun was shining and the birds were singing — I was sitting in a room in the castle reading about Jesu going to the Temple and casting out the moneylenders. Do you remember it? Well, I decided there and then that's what I would do. I called everyone together in the great hall — a huge room it was — I called them all together and ordered them to leave the castle at once, soldiers included. They were so surprised that they all went — in a great procession. It was an extraordinary sight. I remember feeling blissfully happy and, no doubt, much too pleased with myself. Then I sent messages to the peasants asking them to come to the castle the next day. I spoke to them in the courtyard and told them I was going to divide all my father's lands equally between them.'

'Why? The lands were yours.'

'Because that is what our Lord Jesu told us to do. At first, the peasants couldn't believe it. But when they realized I meant what I said they were overjoyed. I left the castle and went to live in an empty hut in the village. And I took my Bible with me — the same one I keep in my box —'

A dark shadow falling across them made Bartholomew stop. He glanced up to see the sun sinking behind the mountains.

'I knew we would never do much picking once I began,' he said, sighing at the small quantities of berries in their baskets. 'Ah well, we'll just have to come again tomorrow.' He got stiffly to his feet. 'Come along, Jan. We must make for the hut before it gets dark.'

'Wait! Don't stop there. Tell me what happened next.'

'I'll tell you the rest when we get home.'

Snorting with frustration and disgust, Stephan scrambled after Bartholomew who was already picking his way down a path among the rocks.

'You can tell me what happened as we walk.'

'No I can't. I need all my breath for walking. And besides, it won't hurt you to learn a little patience.'

As things turned out, Stephan had to curb his impatience for quite a while for, once back at the hut, Bartholomew insisted on completing all the tasks in their regular evening ritual before continuing with his story. The boy raced from one job to the next in an effort to get the old man seated as quickly as possible, while Bartholomew appeared to take longer than usual to deal with the goats. But, at last, with everything done and a pile of fresh logs by the fire, the old man settled on his stool and seemed prepared to speak.

'Well?' Stephan implored. 'What happened next?'

Bartholomew smiled at the glowing impatience of his pupil, then sadly shook his head.

'For a few weeks we lived together in the village,' he said. 'It was very peaceful and, I think, everyone was happy. That huge stone building — the castle — was quite empty, except for stray dogs and rats. Then, one morning I heard horns blowing beyond the village. I looked out and saw soldiers galloping round the huts. They were the same ones I had sent away. And my father's friends were with them. They were shouting and waving swords. I was too shocked to move. I stood in the doorway in a daze watching them kill any peasants who got in their way. They just hacked them down with their swords. And then they started to set light to the huts. It was dreadful. Some of the soldiers spotted me and they began to throw stones at me, yelling that I was a madman. I was terrified. All I could think of was stopping them burning my Bible. I ran inside, picked it up and fled.'

'From the village?'

'Yes. It was cowardly and shameful. But that is what I did.'

Bartholomew was staring at the fire with tears in his eyes.

'Did they hurt you?' Stephan asked gravely.

'A little in my body — but a lot in my soul. I was responsible, you see, for the death of those peasants.'

'No! The soldiers killed them.'

'Yes. But I was responsible too.'

'How?'

'I was foolish enough to think the soldiers wouldn't come back. Some of the peasants warned me it might happen. But I didn't listen.'

'Did you go back to the village?'

'No. I wandered from place to place trying to forget what had happened. But everywhere I went I saw peasants who were hungry and and badly treated, and it kept reminding me of those poor people who had been killed in my village. It made me feel wretched and helpless and, in the end, all I wanted to do was to get away from other people — as far away as possible. So, I came here — to ask God to forgive me.'

'Has he?'

'I believe so.'

For a while, they were both silent, lost in their own thoughts, dimly aware of the fire crackling and the timbers of the roof creaking in the wind. Then, with a bold toss of his head and in a fierce voice, Stephan cried, 'I will fight them. Teach me to use a sword.'

Bartholomew gave a dry chuckle.

'Me? I'm much too old,' he said, throwing a fresh log on the fire. 'Besides, I've forgotten how to do it.'

'Teach me.'

'No, Jan.'

'I will be like the eagle. Teach me!'

'No, Jan.' The old man's voice was stern. 'Let us have no more talk about fighting. The whole idea fills me with horror.'

But Stephan was no longer listening. He was on his feet, alive with the old feelings of strength and confidence imparted by the eagle. Throwing his head back, he uttered a proud, challenging shriek.

20

Bang — crash — bang —
  '— Oh!'

With a look of alarm Bartholomew watched his stick go flying through the air and land on the grass a few yards away.

'Steady on,' he cautioned in a hurt voice, gingerly rubbing the wrist which had been jarred by the impact of Stephan's stick.

'Sorry Bartholomew.'

'You must take it gently. You almost hit me that time.'

Stephan grinned and limped away to retrieve Bartholomew's stick.

'Here you are,' he said, holding out the improvised weapon. 'Sorry if I hurt you.'

'I'm all right — I think. But be careful. There's no need to be so wild. After all, it's only a game. Now it's my turn. Remember what I said. Cut-cut-cut and thrust. Ready?'

Stephan nodded and took guard once more.

His imagination had been so fired by Bartholomew's story that from then on he had done nothing but pester the old man to teach him how to sword-fight. For several days, Bartholomew had remained adamantly against it, refusing to be moved by all Stephan's entreaties. But in the battle of wills it had been the boy's that had won the day and, to keep him quiet, the old man had reluctantly given way.

So, on a cold wintry afternoon, after completing all their chores, they had cut two straight saplings to be their makeshift weapons and, in a misty clearing with the morning's frost still lying on the grass, Bartholomew gave Stephan his first lesson. Much to his surprise, the hermit found he was enjoying it.

They were an ill-matched pair of combatants — a frail, rather shaky old man whose long white beard was tucked into a heavy woollen robe tied with a rope round his waist, and a fair-haired youth who stood half a head taller than his instructor and whose cheeks were ablaze with colour. The old man quickly ran out of breath but he was surprisingly nimble and, so far, had managed to avoid the flailing stick of his handicapped pupil.

'One — two — three — *four!*' And on 'four', Bartholomew nipped forward with his stick and cheekily poked Stephan in the ribs.

'Ha!' Stephan cried. He was disgusted with himself at being caught with his guard hopelessly out of place. 'Now I'm dead.'

'No you're not,' the old man chuckled. 'It's only make-believe. Now it's your turn. But please be careful. Remember my poor eyesight. Are you ready?'

'Ready.'

'One — two — three — *four!*'

Bartholomew stepped smartly back to avoid his opponent's lunge causing Stephan, whose thrust forward had been so uncontrolled and vigorous, to slip and fall flat on his face. The old man laughed merrily like a mischievous child and held out a hand to the boy.

'I can manage,' Stephan said grumpily. He picked himself up and rubbed the shoulder which had taken the impact of his fall on the frozen ground. 'It's *this!*' he exclaimed, angrily hitting his clubbed foot with his stick. 'It makes me fall over.'

Bartholomew smiled compassionately.

'My dear Jan, all you need is practice — you'll see.'

Unfortunately, practice did not bring much improvement — at least, not enough to satisfy Stephan whose impetuous nature was easily discouraged. And after a few more lessons he threw away the stick in despair.

In an effort to take Stephan's mind off what he knew the boy regarded as an abject failure, Bartholomew offered to teach him how to read the Bible. The timing proved to be ideal for within a few days the first heavy falls of snow came which forced them to spend much more time in the shelter of the hut.

On one particularly stormy afternoon they were sitting as usual wrapped in blankets having a reading lesson. The room was full of smoke and the roof timbers creaked and groaned under the pressure of the gale raging outside. The goats moved restlessly in their cramped pen. It had been snowing hard all day and, after bringing in a good supply of logs, they had hardly ventured outside again. Soon it would be dark and Bartholomew rubbed his smarting eyes, yawning a little as Stephan attempted to get his tongue round the unfamiliar text.

Suddenly, the quiet concentration of their studies was interrupted by loud banging on the door. The noise came so unexpectedly that it made them both jump. The Bible slipped from Stephan's knees to the floor, but neither of them moved to retrieve it. They were transfixed by the banging which was still going on. Then, abruptly, it stopped and, a moment later, there was a dull thud of something falling against the door.

The two of them sat very still, staring at the door, waiting for further sounds from outside. But now there was only the howling wind lashing the forest trees. Stephan was the first to move — a sharp turn of his head to look at Bartholomew. He was surprised to see the old man shivering with fright. Thinking it was probably nothing more than a tree that had fallen against the hut, he got up and limped to the door. He turned back for a moment to make sure Bartholomew was all right and saw him gather up the Bible and clasp it with shaking hands to his chest. Boldly, Stephan drew back the wooden bar that secured the door. He had just begun to open it when it was suddenly forced from his hands as a body, covered from head to foot in snow, collapsed across the threshold.

Bartholomew was on his feet at once, all fear forgotten, rushing forward and calling for help to get the body inside. But Stephan seemed unable to respond. He was staring in wide-eyed amazement at the crumpled body and had reverted to making loud hissing noises.

'Stop it!' the old man cried, flaring up in anger. 'It's only a man. He won't hurt you. Stop it!'

The outburst succeeded in quietening the boy and, after more urging from the hermit, he was persuaded to help half-carry, half-drag the unconscious figure into the hut. Telling Stephan to put more logs on the fire, Bartholomew ran back to shut out the blast of freezing air that was blowing flurries of snow over the threshold, and then hurried back to kneel beside the stranger.

In the firelight, they could see the torn, filthy state of the sacking in which the man was swathed. His features were partially hidden beneath a frozen tangle of white hair but, as Bartholomew gently brushed the snow and hair aside, a thin, gaunt face with eyes sunk into dark-rimmed sockets was revealed.

Bartholomew started to rub the man's hands in an attempt to revive him.

'Hot water, Jan,' he whispered. 'We shall need hot water.'

And while Stephan filled a pot with water from the goatskin bag, the hermit continued to rub the man's hands, and then his legs.

The stranger began to stir. His eyelids fluttered and opened, and he tried to focus on the two faces looking down at him. He took a shallow breath and opened his mouth to speak. But no sounds came from his swollen, chapped lips.

'You're safe now,' Bartholomew said with an anxious smile. 'You are among friends.'

There was a grateful look in the stranger's eyes. Then, he gave a little gasp and relapsed into unconsciousness.

'We must get these wet things off,' Bartholomew said to Stephan who had been looking on from a safe distance on the other side of the fire. 'Quickly now.'

Together, they removed the sodden outer layers of sacking and, with further instructions from the hermit, laid the man on Bartholomew's pallet and covered him with a blanket.

116

'Who is this man?' Stephan asked in a disapproving voice, watching Bartholomew wipe the stranger's face with a cloth dipped in warm water.

The hermit shook his head. 'He was lucky to find us,' he said. 'He would have died in the storm.'

They spread the pile of wet sacking round the fire and, while it steamed in the heat, they sat in silence facing the stranger. Bartholomew frequently shook his head and sighed, and Stephan frowned with deep suspicion, trying to assess whether the man who had blundered into their midst was a friend or foe. The desire for sleep finally overtook him and, after returning the forgotten Bible to its box, he retired to his pallet, leaving Bartholomew to sit up with the stranger.

By morning, the blizzard had blown itself out and when Stephan awoke he found everything quiet and still. The stranger was sleeping peacefully and Bartholomew was dozing on his stool by the remains of the fire, with his head on his chest. Stephan gingerly got out of bed, threw a cloak round his shoulders and tip-toed from the hut.

Outside, the snow was deep and the low sun created an uncomfortable glare that made him screw up his eyes. He left deep, irregular footprints as he battled round the hut to get a fresh supply of logs. The snow had drifted against the side of the hut and he had to scoop his way through it to reach the wood under the eaves. He blew on his hands to get them warm again and gathered an armful of logs.

Bartholomew was waiting at the door by the time he returned.

'He's awake,' the old man said, 'but very weak.'

Stephan went into the hut, conscious of the stranger's eyes on him. Weak though he was, the man visibly started at the boy's entrance and, as Stephan limped across the room to the fire, he pointed at the clubbed foot, gasping in an amazed voice, 'He's lame!'

The youth froze and fixed the stranger with a wary stare.

'He's lame! He's lame!' the man kept gasping until, too weak to speak any more, he sank back on the pallet, panting.

Stephan abruptly dropped the logs with a loud clatter and backed away. The noise made Bartholomew jump. He had been concentrating on the man's strange reaction and now saw Stephan shifting his weight from one foot to the other, a sure sign of imminent bird-talk.

'It's all right, Jan,' he said, moving quickly to his pupil.

There was a strangled cry from the pallet. 'Jan? Jan?'

'Yes,' the hermit said guardedly. 'His name is Jan.'

'He lives here?'

'Yes. With me.'

Shaking his head in disbelief, the stranger sank back once more, unable to take his eyes from Stephan, who found the experience distinctly unpleasant.

'I don't like you,' the boy declared in a hard, dismissive voice, and stomped out of the hut.

'He can talk!' the man cried feebly.

'Of course he can talk,' Bartholomew defensively replied. He too was beginning to find the man's behaviour unnerving.

'Is he your son?'

The directness of the question left Bartholomew floundering.

'I must go to him,' he mumbled, turning to go.

'Wait!' The urgency in the voice made Bartholomew hesitate and, at the same time, filled him with sudden apprehension. 'I'm sorry,' the man gasped, 'you must think me ungrateful and rude. Forgive me. But the sight of that lad put everything else from my head. It was a great shock. I even began to hope —!'

'Are you trying to tell me that you know Jan?' Bartholomew slowly asked.

'I'm not sure,' the man admitted with a faraway look in his eyes. 'But he's so like a child I knew once. He's older now, taller. But his hair, his face — so like the child. And being a cripple. It's the same lameness in the right foot. The right foot. I would have said it was the same child. But you tell me he's your son.'

Too distressed to answer, Bartholomew stammered, 'I must find Jan,' and fled from the room.

He stood in the snow with his hands clasped to his mouth, wrestling with emotions that brought tears to his eyes. In his bewildered mind, one fact seemed inescapable — the stranger must be Jan's father.

He had often told himself that one day this might happen but now that it had, he rebelled with every fibre of his body against it. He had looked after the boy, had seen him grow to near manhood. He had taught him — so many things. And there was more to be achieved — Jan's reading had only just begun. He depended on him, loved him and, without realizing it, had come to think of him as his own son.

But a stern, inner voice kept saying, you must tell Jan. In the end, he clasped his hands in a brief prayer in which he tried to praise God for all things — even the pain of giving up the boy — and slowly followed the footprints in the snow.

He found Stephan leaning against a tree near the clearing where they had first met.

'You can't stay out here, Jan,' he said, attempting a brave smile. 'It's too cold. Come back to the hut.'

'I don't like that man,' Stephan replied, moodily kicking at the snow.

'He means you no harm. He has things to tell us.'

'What things?'

'Strange, wonderful things.'

'What things?'

'You must let him tell you.'

'I don't like him.'

'You don't *know* him. Come, please. For my sake.'

Stephan gave him a baleful look and huddled into his cloak.

But, with a little more coaxing, he relented and, holding on to one another, they returned to the hut.

The stranger was dozing as they entered but their presence roused him and Bartholomew resumed his place on the stool. Stephan remained warily apart near the door.

'There is something you should know,' the hermit said gravely. 'Jan is not my son. I don't know who his real father is.'

'Bartholomew is my father,' a loud voice announced from across the room.

'No, Jan. You know as well as I do that I'm not your father.' Bartholomew's voice trembled a little and he hesitated a moment before continuing. 'If I'm not mistaken,' he said, turning to the stranger, 'this is your real father.'

The man gave a wan smile and shook his head.

'I fear you are wrong,' he said. 'I'm not this lad's father.'

'*Not* his father?' In spite of his prayers, Bartholomew's old heart took a leap. 'Then who are you?'

'My name, sir, is Petr.'

21

So Bletz had found its way to the hermit's hut. But the old campaigner of the village was in no state to answer the questions that were crowding the heart and mind of the hermit.

Anyone who had known Petr in the days when he was headman would have been shocked by his appearance now. He had aged, more than the years that had passed. The stocky figure was thin, almost emaciated. The wiry hair and grizzled beard had turned pure white. His face that once had conveyed strength and boldness was now deeply lined.

He had much to tell Bartholomew and Stephan, and they to him. But on that first day with them he could do little except sleep, and the others going quietly about their daily tasks had to contain their impatience, their puzzlement — and fear. The circumstances of the man's coming, his apparent connection with Stephan, the man himself — these, for the time being, were all matters of mystery.

Bartholomew and Stephan were sitting by the light of the fire and a rush dip having a rather muted reading lesson when a feeble voice addressed them from a shadowy corner of the room.

'Can he read?' the voice asked in great surprise.

They turned to see Petr struggling to sit up on the pallet.

'Well, he's learning,' Bartholomew replied with pride.

'Reading — speaking —,' the man sighed, shaking his head in disbelief.

'Put the Bible away, Jan,' the hermit said to keep him busy. 'I think Petr might be ready to take some food.' He got up to look at the gruel which they had kept simmering in a pot over the fire. 'But no questions for the moment,' he added, wagging a finger at the visitor. The rueful look on Petr's face was so open and genuine that it made the hermit chuckle.

Soon Bartholomew was ladling milky oatmeal porridge into three bowls. He handed one to Stephan, who sat with it on the floor near the fire, placed his stool beside Petr and returned with the remaining bowls.

'It's a long time since I've tasted food like this,' Petr said after taking one or two small mouthfuls from the spoon Bartholomew held out for him.

'You were lucky to find us,' the hermit murmured. 'I think God was with you.'

'I never thought to be fed like a baby, though.'

'Be patient. You'll soon be up and about again.'

They smiled at each other and for several moments settled into silence while Bartholomew concentrated on holding the spoon in a rather shaky hand within easy reach of the invalid's mouth. He was finding it a struggle to sip the gruel without spilling it. On the floor, Stephan ate in solemn silence, glancing at the visitor from time to time with dark resentment in his eyes. Petr caught one of these looks and was about to ask a question, and then changed his mind.

'This is good,' he said appreciatively.

'Jan helped me prepare it,' Bartholomew smiled. 'Didn't you, Jan?'

The boy nodded, but refused to be drawn into the conversation.

'He's not usually so quiet,' the hermit tried to explain. 'He's not used to seeing people — neither of us are.'

Petr nodded. 'Has he lived with you long?' he asked.

'Jan was just a child when we first met,' the old man replied with an affectionate look at his pupil.

'Where was that?'

Bartholomew hesitated, wondering if this was the right moment to enlarge on his first encounter with the strange child. Deciding against it, he gestured vaguely towards the door. 'In the forest,' he said. And so as not to seem unhelpful, he added, 'As I recall it was Christmas Day.'

It crossed Petr's mind to ask what year that Christmas Day was in. But events from the past were too muddled in his mind. Instead he asked, 'Could he speak then?'

'Why does he ask so many questions, Bartholomew?' a loud voice from the floor demanded.

'Petr means no harm. He's just curious,' the hermit replied in a conciliatory voice. He turned to the visitor. 'You asked me if Jan could talk when he first came to me. The answer is — no.'

There was a wild look in Petr's eyes. He threw up his hands, crying, 'He *is* the same child!'

'Quietly, my friend. You'll exhaust yourself,' Bartholomew said, looking anxiously at Stephan.

'But you don't know what this means to me. I've been looking for him for months — and now I've found him. Found him!'

In his agitation, Petr flopped back on the pallet, almost knocking the spoon from Bartholomew's hand.

'All in good time,' the old man gently said, aware that Stephan had stopped eating and was glaring at the visitor. 'All in good time. Take some more food.'

'It's very good,' Petr replied, 'but I couldn't eat any more. Thank you.'

'Very well. If you're quite sure.'

Bartholomew put the bowl on the floor and began to eat from his own.

'Let me ask you a question,' he said a little later. 'What relation are you to this child's parents?'

'No blood relation. Only a friend — an old friend. We grew up together in the same village.'

'What village is that?'

'Bletz. It's on the other side of the mountains.' Petr's eyes turned to the boy who had taken himself off to his pallet on the other side of the room. 'Do you remember Bletz?' he asked.

Stephan shook his head and turned his back on the others.

'What is the name of the child you seek?' Bartholomew enquired.

'Stephan.'

'Stephan,' the hermit repeated slowly. There was a faint smile on his face. 'It's a good name. Stephan — the first Christian martyr.'

'Do you remember being called Stephan?' Petr asked.

'My name is Jan,' the youth replied without turning round.

'Jan is the name I gave you,' Bartholomew sighed. 'Wouldn't you like to be called Stephan?' he asked pleasantly.

The question seemed to annoy his pupil who vehemently shook his head.

There was an awkward silence, broken by the hermit saying, 'I think we've had enough questions for one day.' He gave a meaningful look at Petr who nodded agreement.

'There's nothing that can't wait until tomorrow,' Bartholomew said in a cheerful voice that was more for Stephan's benefit than Petr's. 'Rest now, and tomorrow we will talk again.'

He got up and pulled the blanket round the invalid whose eyelids soon began to droop. Not many minutes later, Petr fell into a sleep punctuated by hectic dreams in which it was never clear if he was the pursuer, or the pursued.

'You mustn't be so hard on him,' Bartholomew whispered sternly when he was sure the visitor was asleep.

'I wish he hadn't come,' Stephan moodily replied.

'I know. But he's here. And we must praise God for bringing him to us.' The old man did his best to sound reassuring but he, too, was troubled by thoughts of what Petr might have in store for them.

The following day saw a noticeable improvement in the invalid. He felt rested and there was even a little colour in his cheeks. He had woken up with a head full of questions, but it was his turn to be patient. He lay on the pallet watching the boy coming in and out of the hut going about his daily chores, convinced that this was Josef and Marta's child. By the time the others were seated with him, he could barely contain his excitement.

'Do you remember your father?' he began eagerly.

Stephan shook his head.

'Or your mother?'

'He can remember nothing of his childhood,' Bartholomew said.

'Not even his father or mother?'

'Nothing at all.'

Petr frowned, and tried again.

'Do you remember the cave?' he asked.

Stephan's head came up sharply. 'A cave?' For the first time he sounded genuinely interested and it made the others look at him expectantly.

'Yes, a cave — in the mountains,' Petr replied, hoping that at last he had found something the lad could remember from those far-off days. 'Your father took you there.'

The remark seemed to make Stephan withdraw into himself and he slowly shook his head.

'Are you sure you don't remember the cave?' Petr persisted.

'No!' the youth angrily shouted.

'Perhaps, it would be best, Petr, if you just tell us what you know,' Bartholomew's gentle voice suggested.

'Very well,' Petr shrugged. He looked directly at Stephan who was frowning at him from his usual place on the floor.

'I know it's difficult for you to understand,' he began, 'but I honestly believe your real name is Stephan. I was there in the church when your father gave the name to the priest.'

'Bartholomew is my father,' the youth stated in a voice that was like a stone wall.

'No, Jan. It's no good talking like this. I'm not your father. Now, listen to what Petr has to say.'

'Your father, Stephan —'

'Jan!' the youth screamed.

'Very well — Jan. It's just hard for me to think of you as anything except Stephan. But I'll try to remember to call you Jan. Your father — Jan — was a woodman. He was a bondsman to the Lord of Bletz. Josef, your father, was a good man. A kind, loving man who was always good to Marta — your mother — and you.'

'You speak of things that are past,' Bartholomew's anxious voice remarked. 'Is Josef dead?'

'No, not exactly. But when I last had news of him, he was living like one who is dead.'

'What do you mean?'

Petr hesitated. He had not intended to talk about this — at least, not so soon.

'What has happened to Josef?' the hermit was asking.

The visitor sighed and in a grim voice said, 'He's a prisoner. In the castle of Bletz.'

Bartholomew's hand instinctively went to his crucifix.

'And Josef's wife?' he asked tremulously.

'Marta still lives — I hope. But if she does, it will be alone, in the dwelling where Stephan — I'm sorry, Jan — was born.'

'You said this Josef is good,' Stephan said in a disdainful way. 'Why is he in prison?'

The question was asked in such a demanding tone that it made Petr, the staunch friend of Josef and Marta, feel suddenly angry that their child should have so little feeling for them.

'He was put there by evil men,' he replied tartly.

'There are many evil men in the world,' the youth said loftily. 'Bartholomew has told me about them.'

The hermit, who knew this haughty tone only too well, was about to rebuke his pupil but, deciding it was better to hold his peace, addressed a question to Petr instead. 'Why was Josef put into prison?' he asked.

'I hesitate to tell you. It's very distressing.'

'It will not distress me,' a belligerent voice declared. 'I'm not afraid. I'm not even afraid of *you*,' the boy added with a challenging stare at Petr.

'Jan, stop it,' Bartholomew remonstrated. 'Petr is our guest. He's not trying to frighten you. He just doesn't want to upset you.'

'Well let him tell us. Then we'll see.'

Stephan tossed his head in a way that made the hermit's heart sink, and glared at Petr who was finding it hard to reconcile the helpless child that he had last seen with this difficult, argumentative youth.

'Please tell us,' Bartholomew said with an apologetic smile.

'Go on, tell us.'

'Jan, if you can't be quiet, you'll have to go outside.' With ill grace, Stephan hung his head, but seemed prepared to allow Petr to speak.

'Many years ago,' Petr began, 'I was exiled by the Lord of Bletz. My wife and I went to live in the forest some distance from the village. I won't go into the reasons for this punishment now — it would take too long to explain. The important thing is that no one was allowed to visit us. And no one did — except Josef and Marta. I tried to tell them not to do it, but they insisted on coming. One day last summer, they were followed by one of the men in the village. An unpleasant man — the carpenter at Bletz. He told the headman — a villain if ever there was one — and that man told the Lord. The same day, soldiers took Josef and Marta to the castle where they were cruelly beaten. Your mother, Jan, was allowed to go home. But your father was put in prison.'

'Dear Lord in Heaven,' Bartholomew murmured under his breath, 'was that their only crime?'

Petr nodded. 'The Lord of Bletz is a tyrant.'

'How did you learn this?' the hermit asked in a shocked voice.

'The next day, soldiers came to the forest after me. They burned my shelter and everything I possessed. Mercifully, my wife had died two winters before. They joked and bragged about what they had done to Josef and Marta. It was almost dark by the time they rode off and I vowed there and then that I would try to find Stephan — Jan. You see, his parents thought he was dead. But I wouldn't — couldn't — accept it. My wife always said that I'm a stubborn man. And I suppose I am.'

Petr gave a little cough to clear the constriction in his throat. Aware of the silence in the room, he glanced at the hermit, who was staring into space with tears in his eyes, and then at Stephan. The boy seemed to have withdrawn into a private world that was remote and unapproachable. Beneath a heavy frown his eyes glinted with a ferocity that sent a shiver down Petr's back. Suddenly, there was a deafening shriek and, before anyone could move, Stephan had rushed from the hut.

Unable to believe the evidence of his ears, Petr turned in bewilderment to Bartholomew for an explanation. But the old man could only shake his head and sigh. They listened in silence to the shrieks growing fainter as Stephan blundered away through the snow. And at last, as though by way of an answer, Bartholomew said, 'We have much to tell you.'

'Did I do that to him?' Petr asked in alarm.

'No, my friend, you're not to blame. It was bound to happen sooner or later. That is Jan — or Stephan — or both.' Bartholomew got up to put fresh logs on the fire. 'I don't know yet how Jan — you see, I still think of him by that name — I don't know yet how he came to be separated from his parents. Any more than you know how he comes to cry like an eagle — yes, it is an eagle. But all in good time, my friend. Be content for the present that your long search is over.'

22

They left in the spring, when the streams were in flood and the floor of the forest was carpeted with flowers — wind flowers, violets, celandines, primroses, wild orchids in the most sheltered places and already the young heads of bluebells washing the other colours with the faintest of blue hazes.

Stephan and Petr left — Bartholomew remained behind. In spite of all the young man's entreaties and arguments, the hermit stubbornly maintained that he had taken a vow to live apart from other men and he would not break it now. Secretly he hoped that something would prevent Stephan from leaving but, in his heart, he had known from the day of Petr's arrival that his pupil would go.

During the weeks of winter, he saw Stephan's distrust and resentment of Petr change to an intense curiosity that made him ask to hear again and again the story of how he came to be separated from his parents. As far as Bartholomew could tell, it was not an attempt to rekindle feelings of love for his parents, who he continued to call 'Josef' and 'Marta', never Father and Mother. But rather it was to relive the feelings that were expressed in the look of fierce pride on his face and which sometimes exploded into action, making him strut about the room proclaiming the end of all evil men in Bletz. Bartholomew frequently warned him against the sin of revenge and Petr tried to explain that revenge was a practical impossibility. But their words seemed to make little impact on Stephan, except to drive him from the hut, shrieking and squawking.

'Does he think he is an eagle?' Petr asked on one of these occasions when the two men were alone in the hut listening to the strange cries in the forest.

'At times like these, I think he must,' Bartholomew admitted.

Bartholomew had always loved the spring, but this year he dreaded its coming. On the morning of departure he did his best to be cheerful, saying he was positively looking forward to some peace and quiet, and urging the others to be on their way. But as he stood in the doorway watching them walk away, the sight of Stephan with a heavy burden on his back limping eagerly beside Petr, who was equally laden, was more than he could bear. He went into the hut and, falling on his knees, prayed for the safe-keeping of his pupil and the boy's guide, and to be given strength to bear his loneliness.

For the first few days the weather was kind to the travellers. The sun shone on their faces, they drank water from freezing streams and ate food from the bundles of provisions. By night, they slept wrapped in blankets beside a fire to keep away the wolves. Stephan was filled with boundless energy and would have marched all day if Petr had not insisted on taking an occasional rest.

After five days of trekking through the forest, they emerged from the trees to find themselves facing barren rocks. Above, and beyond them, were soaring peaks, many covered in snow. It had been a hard morning's climb and Petr called a halt. He rested on a rock, shivering in the chill wind, and looked at Stephan who, as usual, refused to sit down. The boy was looking intently at the sky, searching perhaps for a familiar silhouette against the scurrying clouds. Petr shook his head in silent wonder at the thought of the youth being carried as a child by an eagle.

He still found it hard to equate this strange, often uncomfortable boy with Josef and Marta's child. During the weeks and months spent wandering in the mountains, the picture he had always had in his mind was of a child, unable to speak, crying in his father's arms. What would Marta make of her son now? Or Josef? He hardly dared to think what might have happened to his old friend.

He got stiffly to his feet and called, 'Time to move on, Jan.'

That evening the weather closed in and, after an uncomfortable night among the rocks, they woke to find the mountains shrouded in a freezing mist.

The bad weather stayed with them for three days, slowing down their progress and making the climb which at the best times would have been difficult, extremely treacherous. The nights were bitterly cold and wet and, for the first time, Stephan's spirits began to flag.

They had been struggling up a narrow gorge for what seemed like hours to Stephan when he stopped and shouted angrily to Petr who was climbing ahead. Drenched by the spray thrown up by a river as it crashed against huge boulders in its wake, and cursing the dead weight of his clubbed foot that constantly slipped on the wet rocks, he yelled at him to stop or find an easier route. But his guide simply waved him on and resumed climbing.

Surrounded by flurries of snow that had been falling for much of the day, Stephan searched the grey void before him, hoping that by some miracle he would see the eagle flying towards him. For a few dream-like moments he was back in those exhilarating days of flight — the days when the journey over the mountains had been so effortless. The weight of the straps on his shoulders were replaced by the grip of the eagle's talons. The gale became the rush of the wind blowing his hair as his mind took him out into space.

He was brought back to earth by distant shouts and, looking up, he saw Petr excitedly waving to him to catch up. Groaning inwardly, he brushed the wet snow from his face and resumed the disagreeable task of scrambling up the rocks.

Petr was waiting for him with an arm outstretched to pull him up the last few paces.

'We've made it!' his guide shouted above the wind. 'This is the highest point in the journey. From now on it's all downhill. But be careful.' Petr smiled encouragingly and turned to go. Then something in the youth's expression made him hesitate.

'You all right?' he asked gruffly.

'Of course.'

'You're not afraid?'

'I'm not afraid of anything.'

The lofty reply which would have irritated Petr on another occasion, now made him chuckle. For all the lad's arrogance there was something very vulnerable, likeable, about him.

'You are your father's son,' he said, clasping Stephan's shoulders in a bear-like hug. He had embraced Josef like that before leaving to take the child into hiding.

The night was colder and more miserable than any they had yet encountered. They slept very little and were ready to continue the descent at first light. The gradients were often steep and icy and, on all sides, the drops were perilous. But with Petr leading the way and always ready to offer a guiding hand, they slowly clambered down the mountain side.

As the day wore on and the high altitudes were left behind, the weather began to improve. The thick clouds and mist slowly lifted and by late afternoon, as they scrambled down a steep scree, the sun suddenly came out, flooding the valley below them in yellow light. With a gleeful whoop, Stephan broke into a lop-sided run, slipping and sliding on the loose stones. Heedless of Petr's shouts to take care, he went careering down the slope with his bundle banging from side to side across his back until, to Petr's relief, he slid to a breathless stop at the bottom.

They camped for the night beside a small lake where they found enough wood to make a modest fire. They removed the sodden outer layers of sacking and laid them over rocks to dry and, for the first time in several days, ate with relish. They were both weary, dirty and dishevelled, but they could relax in the knowledge that the worst of the journey was over. Later, with blankets round their shoulders, they sat by the fire as darkness slowly closed in around them.

'Was that the way you came when you were looking for me?' Stephan asked soberly.

Petr nodded.

'How did you remember?'

'You forget, I spent many weeks in these mountains. I got to know them very well.

'Bartholomew says it was a miracle you found us. Do you think it was a miracle?'

'Perhaps.'

Stephan studied his companion with that disconcerting stare of his.

'Why did you look for me?' he asked. 'You said Josef thought I was dead.'

'You must not blame your father for that. Any man would have thought the same.'

'But you did not.'

'No. It's hard to explain why. Call it stubbornness if you like.'

'Bartholomew says God told you to look for me. Did God tell you?'

'I'll confess something to you, Jan, that I could never tell Bartholomew. He is a man of great faith — and I envy him. I don't believe in God. I've tried. And when I was a young man, like you, I thought I believed. But I've seen evil men triumph too often over people who are innocent and helpless. And I can't believe in a God who allows that.'

'You cannot blame God. That is men's doing.'

'Is that Bartholomew talking — or you?'

'I say, I will fight them.'

'Jan, listen to me. You can't fight soldiers — remember what happened to Bartholomew.'

'Batholomew did not have the eagle.'

'Do you really think the eagle can help you? You've not seen it for many years. By now, it may even be dead.'

'You did not believe I was dead.'

The unanswerable logic of this made Petr laugh. 'I see Bartholomew has brought you up to be a philosopher,' he chuckled. He looked at the boy sitting so upright and still, and his face grew serious.

'Is that why you've come?' Petr asked suddenly. 'In the hope of seeing the eagle again?'

'Yes.'

The utter confidence in the voice made Petr sigh. 'And I thought it was to see your mother,' he said.

'I would like to see Marta — and Josef.'

'Your mother, perhaps. But not your father, Jan. You must try to reconcile yourself to that.'

'I want to see them both.'

Feeling slightly irritated, but knowing that further argument would get them nowhere, Petr shrugged and threw the last remaining sticks on the dwindling fire.

'Time we turned in for the night,' he said. 'There's a long march ahead of us tomorrow.'

By mid afternoon they reached the cave where so many years before Josef had taken his son into hiding. Before going inside, Petr took Stephan to the promontory overlooking the waterfall where he hoped to be able to give him his first, though distant, view of Bletz. But low cloud obscured the view and there was little to be seen except the misty shapes of tree tops. Trying not to feel disappointed, Petr led Stephan to the cave, standing aside to let him go in first. With growing anticipation, he watched the youth limping round, touching the walls and the ceiling. He had a curious impression that the place was smaller than he remembered, but came to the conclusion that it was simply because Stephan had grown.

'Your father always had to stoop to get in,' he said, hoping to draw a response. Stephan nodded and limped further into the cave.

A few moments later there was an angry shout as Stephan

stumbled against a rock in the darkness and he reappeared, rubbing a bruised knee.

'It smells damp back there,' he said, making a face.

Petr was disappointed.

'Is this really the cave where Josef left me?' the boy asked.

The implied criticism of the question, and the tone of disapproval in Stephan's voice, combined to make Petr too angry to reply. So much pain, so much effort, so much danger, he thought, and the boy doesn't seem to care.

'Well?' he asked impatiently. 'Do you remember it?'

'I'm not sure,' Stephan replied after a moment's thought. 'Perhaps. But I will remember it now,' he added with a maddening smile.

Petr snorted with frustration. He had hoped for so much more and, for a while, tried to prod Stephan's memory by describing the visit he had made with the woodman. But those days of childhood when Stephan and the hare had run away to hide at the rear of the cave were locked away in a past that had gone for ever.

They sat in the cave eating a late lunch from their diminishing supplies while Petr talked about the visit to Marta.

'I'll go alone first,' he said. 'It will be a great shock to your mother to learn you're still alive and I must prepare her gently. It's too dangerous to visit her in daylight, so I'll wait in the forest until it's dark. I'll come back here early tomorrow morning and, if all is well, we'll go together in the evening. While I'm gone, you must not wander from the cave. Promise me.'

The light was already beginning to fade as he climbed down beside the waterfall. He gave a brief wave to Stephan, who was watching from the top, and hurried away.

Stephan sat down on a rock, idly looking at the water falling into the dark pool at the bottom. His thoughts flitted between Bartholomew, whom he knew and loved; Petr, whom he had grown to like and trust; and the parents whom he knew only by their names. He tried to picture himself living in the cave — but drew a blank. He was puzzled that, in his mind, it was associated, not with Josef, but the eagle. His eyes went to the sky and, for a few moments, he tried to will the great bird to appear. He got up and, as he had done so many times in the past, he called. And, as ever, there was no reply. A gust of chill wind blowing across the mouth of the cave made him shiver and, disconsolately, he went inside.

But his cries had not gone unnoticed. Facing into the wind, motionless, the golden eagle had been appraising the tiny figure by the waterfall. It was too high for any human eye to pick it out as a dark speck against the louring clouds, or see its huge wings flap as it began its flight back to the eyrie.

It was still a creature of majesty but, as it landed on the ledge, it was panting slightly and the colours of the feathers ruffled by the wind had faded. The voice that shrieked had lost some of its old power. But the message was clear — I am watching!

23

Petr walked steadily towards the waterfall and for the first time since leaving the forest, he stopped, chest heaving, hands on hips. He glanced back at the way he had just come, and then at the glistening cascade of water. It was cool in the shadow of the high cliff but he had been going since dawn and he was sweating. With the water thundering in his ears, he suddenly felt tired and old.

'I must be mad,' he muttered to himself. Grunting, he knelt down and splashed his face with the freezing water from the pool.

He half expected to be met at the top by Stephan but the promontory was deserted and he called towards the cave. The lack of response made him frown and he went inside, only to find it deserted. Blankets and open bundles were strewn about, but there was no sign of Stephan. It was all too reminiscent of that occasion in the past when he had come with Josef. Cursing under his breath, he hurried outside and shouted again.

In his present mood, it was irritation more than relief that he felt when a familiar voice hailed him from a little way up the mountain side. Stephan was scrambling down towards him, waving happily.

'I told you to stay here,' he said as the youth approached.

'I was only exploring.'

Petr grunted and went into the cave to sit down.

'Well?' Stephan asked, sitting beside him.

'Well, what?'

'Did you see Marta?'

'Yes.'

'And?'

Petr looked at the eager face of his companion and grudgingly admitted to himself that it was unreasonable to be cross simply because the lad had strayed a little way from the cave. Putting his ill-humour down to weariness, he said, 'Yes, I've seen your mother, Jan. She's overjoyed at the thought of seeing you tonight.'

'Do we have to wait so long? Why can't we go now?'

'Because it's too dangerous. Besides, I haven't slept and it's a long way for an old man. Let me rest and then I'll tell you about it.'

Petr gathered a blanket round him and lay down with his back to Stephan. The meeting with Marta had been emotionally exhausting and the hours spent in the forest waiting for the dawn had been unpleasantly cold and damp. But more than this, the months spent in the mountains had permanently weakened his old resilience and strength. Before long he was fast asleep, snoring.

It was several hours before he woke and he found Stephan still sitting where he had last seen him. It looked as though the boy had not moved. Seeing him awake, Stephen grinned and, in his most winning way, began to plead with him.

'Don't make us wait until evening, Petr. Say we can go soon. Please. We don't have to see Marta before it's dark. We could wait in the forest. No one will see us. I promise to do everything you tell me. *Please.*'

It was impossible to resist. Petr made a half-hearted attempt at a protest, but it was more for the sake of appearances than anything else and he soon capitulated.

They ate the last of the food they had brought with them, gathered everything together and, with the bundles on their backs, set out from the cave.

From a high crag, the ever-vigilant eagle saw them leave. It had taken up temporary residence shortly after dawn, but it was in no hurry to follow, knowing that it could easily catch up with the travellers on foot — if it so desired. For the moment, it was more interested in warming itself in the sunshine.

It was late afternoon, and still quite light, by the time the travellers approached the forest boundary. They could see the woodman's dwelling a short distance ahead and Petr called a halt. Forgetting all his promises to the contrary, Stephan begged his guide to go on. But this time Petr remained firm.

'If you won't think of your own safety,' he said sternly, 'think of your mother's. It would be the end of everything if anyone found us there.'

'But who will come?'

'Listen to me, Jan. You don't know about these things — I do. And I tell you there is danger everywhere. Now, we'll have no more arguments. We'll wait here until it's dark.'

Finding a well-hidden vantage point among the ferns and brambles, they took off the bundles and settled in to wait for nightfall.

Stephan sat with his eyes glued to the small dwelling that had once been his home. It looked forlorn and empty. The thatch was in need of repair and the pile of logs and saplings standing near by had clearly been there for many months from the moss growing over them and the decayed state of the ones at the bottom. He supposed Marta was inside but the only sign of movement was a thin column of smoke silently rising from the roof which, from time to time, wafted in their direction. The sweet smell of woodsmoke made Stephan think of the hermit's hut.

A picture of that familiar scene with the goats tethered outside and the stream running through the clearing floated into his mind. He tried to imagine what Bartholomew might be doing at that moment. He rather wished the hermit was with him now to ease the strange nervousness he felt at meeting Marta. He frowned, drew himself upright, and looked at the patch of sky visible through the branches. He saw large clouds beginning to gather, but nothing else.

Petr, who was sitting at his elbow watching his every move, saw this upward glance, and knew exactly what was going through his mind. Not for the first time, it made him doubt the wisdom of this forthcoming meeting.

On his visit the night before, he had found Marta very frail. He had almost been afraid to tell her that her son was still alive. At first, she did not believe it, but when he finally convinced her that it was so, she cried for a long time. He tried to warn her that her son was no longer the child she had known, though he had not been able to bring himself to mention the eagle. The eagle! His thoughts so often returned to that creature he had never seen. It was so hard to believe. And yet what other explanation could there be for the weird sounds coming from the boy's lips? He shook his head and, quite involuntarily, looked at the sky where, for an instant, he thought he saw a dark shape wheeling among the clouds. Before he could collect himself, he was jolted back to earth by a hand gripping his arm.

He glanced at Stephan and then in the direction to which the boy nodded. In the distance, beyond the oak trees, was an unmistakably familiar figure.

'Lobvic!' Petr exclaimed under his breath. And feeling Stephan stiffen beside him, he put out a restraining hand.

They watched the carpenter jog towards the dwelling looking like a grotesque bird with his spindly legs and a piece of sacking that flapped round his shoulders. The man paused for a moment, no doubt to draw breath, and then banged on the door. It took several more knocks before the door was slowly opened.

'Your mother,' Petr whispered.

Stephan inched forward to get a better view of the figure standing in the threshold. Never having seen a woman before, he was intrigued by her clothes and he was surprised to see how small she looked, especially beside the gangling figure of the carpenter who nonchalantly leaned against the door post as he talked to Marta. She was too far away for Stephan to see her face clearly, but he had an impression of pale skin surrounded by grey hair that was plaited close to her head. He strained to hear what was being said, but the words remained unintelligible. He heard the man's laughter and could sense the distress it caused to Marta. After a while, the carpenter pushed his way inside and, with obvious reluctance, she followed. The door was closed, and a tense silence fell on the scene.

'What's he up to?' Petr growled, voicing his thoughts aloud.

They stared at the dwelling, waiting for the moment when the door would reopen. Suddenly there was a terrible cry from inside. It was Marta's voice and it came so unexpectedly that it made the two onlookers jump. For a moment Petr relaxed his grip on Stephan, who immediately leaped to his feet and went crashing away through the undergrowth. He was out in the open before Petr could catch up with him, blundering towards the pile of logs. He seized a sapling from the top and started shrieking louder than Petr, who was desperately trying to reach him, had ever heard before.

The noise brought Lobvic from inside and, before he could move or defend himself, a mighty swing of the pole struck him on the head and he toppled over.

It was all over in an instant and it brought Petr to an abrupt halt. He stared aghast at the carpenter who was lying very still with blood gushing from an open wound. Running forward again, he knelt beside the man and found to his horror that Lobvic was dead.

In a sudden rage, Petr stood up and charged the youth who was performing a mad dance, squawking and swinging the pole about his head. Yelling at him to stop, he made a grab for the pole and, after a tussle in which he became a partner in the wild dance, he succeeded in wrenching it out of Stephan's hands. He threw it on the ground and they, too, fell together in a confusion of thrashing limbs.

'You fool! You fool!' Petr shouted, gaining the upper hand and pinning Stephan to the ground. 'You've killed him!'

'Petr?' a voice called. 'Is that you?'

The two combatants paused in their struggle to see Marta in the doorway.

'Yes, it's me,' Petr panted. He disentangled himself from Stephan and got shakily to his feet.

There was a cry of shock as Marta saw the dead carpenter. She swayed and reached out for the door. Thinking she was going to faint, Petr ran to give support.

'I thought I heard screeching — a bird,' she murmured in a daze.

'There was no bird,' Petr grimly replied. He saw her looking in bewilderment at Stephan and, with a sinking heart, said, 'This is your son. I fear he's killed the carpenter.'

She broke away from Petr and ran unsteadily towards Stephan who was shifting his weight from foot to foot. For a moment, mother and son looked at one another in silence. Then, in a voice full of wonder and sorrow, Marta asked, 'Are you really my son? Are you really Stephan?'

'My name is Jan,' the youth said warily.

'He thinks his name is Jan,' Petr tried to explain. 'But there's no doubt — he is your son.'

Hearing this, Marta threw her arms round Stephan, and wept. The boy was unsure what to do. He looked at Petr for guidance, but the grim face told him nothing. The trembling arms and heaving sobs in the soft, frail body, so close to his, seemed to demand comfort and, in an abrupt, awkward movement, he folded his arms around his mother.

Standing a little apart, Petr thought, 'He has returned, as he left, surrounded by tears.'

In the gathering dusk, the two men carried Lobvic's body into the forest. They worked silently, methodically, covering it with earth and bracken until a brief nod from Petr signalled that he was satisfied. Still without exchanging a word, they walked slowly away from the scene of their labours. The body might never be found but Petr knew it would not be long before the carpenter was missed. So far, there had been no opportunity to ask Marta the reason for the man's visit, but it was not hard to guess that the blacksmith had a hand in it. Perhaps, even now, Hans was waiting for his crony.

They returned to the dwelling to find Marta much calmer. She was stirring a pot of broth and, as they entered, she looked up and smiled.

'It's a poor offering,' she said. 'But you must both be hungry. Sit down. It'll soon be ready.'

She made no reference to the carpenter and whatever questions were on the tip of Petr's tongue were kept to himself. He sat on a stool at the table on which a rush dip flickered and watched Stephan restlessly limping round the room, peering into all the corners. He wondered whether it was just curiosity, or whether the boy was looking for evidence of his childhood. All that — the real reason for their visit — had been pushed to one side by the sudden death of the carpenter.

'We can't stay long,' Petr said, breaking the silence.

'I know,' Marta replied with simple resignation.

They caught each other's eyes and silently acknowledged what they both knew — Stephan would have to go away and, perhaps, never return.

'I want to see Josef,' the youth announced, stepping into the light of the fire.

'That's impossible,' Petr retorted.

'I will go to the castle and demand to see him.'

'It's impossible. Your father's in prison and you have killed a man.'

'He was an evil man.'

'That's beside the point. You have placed yourself — and your mother — in danger of your lives. Hasn't she suffered enough?' The words were spilling out of Petr in a hoarse, angry tirade. 'You must go away from here. Go back where you came from.' He waved vaguely in the direction of the mountains. 'Go back to Bartholomew. Just go away — and leave your mother in peace.'

His anger spent, Petr buried his face in his hands, muttering in a tormented voice, 'I should never have brought you. I'm a fool. A meddling fool.'

The object of his anger frowned at him, stiff and silent. Marta, who had been listening in shocked silence with the spoon poised in her hand, now unhooked the pot from the fire and placed it on the floor. She moved quietly to Petr and lightly touched him on the shoulder.

'Don't blame yourself, Petr,' she said. 'I'm glad you brought my son back to me. He's right, Lobvic was an evil man. I'm sorry it had to be my son who killed him. But I'm not sorry he is dead.'

She turned and looked at the youth by the fire. She thought he looked handsome and strong. She would have liked to have had time to get to know him but, with a mother's instinct, she wondered whether that would have been possible.

'Stephan — Jan — whichever name you prefer — you must go as soon as you've eaten,' she said gently. 'You can't see your father. Even if Lobvic was still alive, you couldn't see your father. It's too late.'

'What do you mean, too late?'

'Things are very bad in the village — perhaps, Petr has told you. We're all hungry. Many are sick. Each week there are more deaths. Once we had Petr to speak for us. Now, we have no one. And not even Petr could help us now.'

'What are you trying to tell us, Marta?' Petr looked up in alarm.

'Some of the men planned an uprising. That's what the carpenter came to tell me. He boasted he discovered it himself. He said it was his duty to tell the headman. That scoundrel. Hans no doubt told the Lord, and this morning the men were rounded up and taken to the castle. Count Boleslav sentenced them to be burned tomorrow.'

'And Josef?'

Tears welled up in Marta's eyes and she shook her head, unable to speak.

'What about Josef?' Petr insisted. 'We heard you scream. Was it something to do with Josef?'

'He'll die with the others,' Marta sobbed with her hands over her mouth.

For Petr, who knew Stephan, the shriek that followed should have been predictable, inevitable. But for Marta it left her staring in wide-eyed astonishment at her son. She was only dimly aware of the fire spluttering as a sudden squall brought spits of rain falling through the hole in the roof. But when the rain began to find its way through the weakest patches of thatch, she was forced to rouse herself and deal with the drips falling on the floor. She hurried round the room with pots and dishes, knowing exactly where to place them for she had done it many times before.

Petr, who had been silently staring into space, unmoved by shrieks or the rain, slowly raised an arm and, in a violent gesture that extinguished the rush dip, brought his fist down on the table with a crash.

'It's time to put an end to this,' he vowed. 'We'll go together,' he added, knowing the boy would never allow him to go alone.

'The eagle will help us,' Stephan declared with a toss of his head.

In the semi-darkness, the rain fell into the earthenware vessels, splashing over the rims to create rings of dampness on the earth floor.

24

S leep would not come to Hans. Even the restless, haunted
sleep that he was now used to evaded him. He had waited
for Lobvic long into the night and in the end, still furious with
the carpenter, he had lain down, fully dressed, on his pallet.

Hans wanted to be sure that Lobvic had carried out his
orders and gone to the woodman's dwelling. Above all, he
desired the satisfaction of hearing that Marta's spirit had been
finally broken by news of her husband's imminent execution.
After all, he had engineered it — admittedly with the priest's
help.

They made a good combination, Father Vilem and himself.
He kept his ear to the ground and the priest always had the
right words for persuading the Lord of Bletz to do what they
wanted. The priest seemed content to grow ever fatter, and
Hans had wood for the fire and enough food for himself and his
family, which was more than could be said of any other
family. Life was a battle for survival and, as only the strongest
survived, he would never cease to fight to be the strongest —
whatever the consequences. It was overhearing some peasants
admiring the woodman's bravery that had driven him to get
rid of the man once and for all.

Dawn found him already on his feet, banging his arms
across his chest to get warm and scowling at the rain falling on
the clods of earth over the fire. For all his advancing years, he
remained an ox of a man and his tangle of black hair was only
just beginning to show streaks of grey.

His family was still asleep as he went to the door and looked
out. The rain falling steadily outside made him wonder for a
moment whether the burnings would be delayed. Then two
figures steadily walking up the muddy track took his attention. From the heavy burdens on their backs and the wet
sacking over their heads and shoulders they looked like

travellers. One seemed to be an old man, the other, younger, was a cripple.

Hans hung back in the doorway until they were almost level with him, then he stepped out to confront them. With grim satisfaction, he noticed that his sudden appearance startled them.

'A vile morning,' he said, trying to see the faces under the rough hoods.

'Specially for travellers,' the older of the two muttered. He held one end of the hood across his face so that only his eyes were visible.

'Are you from hereabouts?'

'We're strangers,' the cripple said, revealing his face and staring at Hans with a candour that annoyed the blacksmith.

'Have you come far?'

'Far enough,' the hidden voice grunted.

Hans scowled. There was something vaguely familiar about the gruff voice but he could not place it.

'What village is this?' the cripple was asking.

'Bletz,' Hans replied with his eyes still on the hooded face.

'And what place is that?' the youth enquired, pointing to the stone fortress on the hill.

'The castle of Bletz. The home of Count Boleslav.'

'Perhaps we'll find shelter there.'

The blacksmith gave a derogatory chuckle. 'I think not. Strangers are not welcome in Bletz — specially today.'

'What's so special about today?'

'We've got executions.'

'Hangings?'

'No. Burnings.'

'We've seen many things on our travels, but never burnings. I would like to see these burnings.'

'I've told you, strangers are not welcome in Bletz. Take it from me, they won't let you into the castle.'

'Is that where the burnings will take place?'

'You come asking a lot of questions.'

'He's only curious,' the gruff voice said. 'He means no harm.'

'Then take my advice and move on. This is no place for strangers.'

'You speak with authority,' the hooded man said. 'As one who knows about these things.'

'I do,' the blacksmith bragged with an arrogant tilt to his beard. 'I'm the headman of Bletz.'

'Then you disappoint us,' the traveller remarked, restraining the cripple who had made a sudden lurch forward.

'What d'you mean, disappoint? No one tells me what to do. I come and go as I please.. And I can have unwelcome strangers thrown out.'

'And deny us the chance of seeing something new? Something we've not seen in all our long travels? If your word carries as much weight as you claim, surely you can get us into the castle? Go on, give the lad a chance to join in the fun. Give us both a day to remember.'

The request — or challenge — was put in such a way that Hans had to accede to it or lose face. He agreed and saying that he would meet them at the bridge, he went back inside his hut.

While they waited for the blacksmith, a steady stream of peasants passed them on their way up to the castle. Many were people that Petr recognized and he longed to answer their enquiring looks by throwing off his disguise and greeting them. He was horrified and angered at their starved faces and torn, dirty clothes and, by the time Hans rejoined them, it needed all Petr's self-control to maintain the pretence of being a stranger.

Shouting to the guards, 'They're with me,' the blacksmith led them through the gates and into the courtyard where he promptly left them to speak to Vislav who had just entered. The irony that it had been Hans, of all people, who had given them safe conduct into the castle made Petr chuckle. Indeed, the first hurdle had been surmounted with such surprising ease that he was almost tempted to offer thanks to the God he did not believe in.

Petr found it very strange to be standing in the courtyard again after such a long absence — the high stone walls and the muddy cobbles under his feet were so familiar. It was as though the missing years had been nothing but a dream. He could not remember ever having seen the courtyard look so crowded. The whole district was there — villagers, peasants from outlying farms, young and old, even babes in arms.

They had come no doubt on the orders of Count Boleslav, but it was clear that, in their own minds, they were there to give support to the poor men about to die. It was their silence which most impressed Petr. It seemed they had agreed with one accord to express their bitter resentment by not speaking — even the cries of the babies were muted. Like arms protecting a body, they filed silently into the castle and surrounded the huge scaffold of kindling wood and timber that stood in the centre of the courtyard.

Petr tried to spot Marta in the crowd. They had decided it would be safer if she came separately, and he had seen her enter. But now she was lost in the sea of faces. He heard Hans' and Vislav's harsh voices demanding if anyone had seen the carpenter and he hoped they would not find Marta.

Standing beside him, Stephan's eyes constantly moved between the sky and the courtyard. He could not help feeling excited at the sight of so large a building. It made him think of the castle Bartholomew had once lived in. Even the soldiers in their metal helmets and chain mail were just as the hermit had described them. His hand felt for the axe he had taken from the woodman's dwelling and which now lay hidden in the bundle at his feet. Then his eyes returned to the sky, and his heart ached at its emptiness.

A shouted command from a sergeant-at-arms went echoing round the walls and, a few moments later, the great wooden doors were closed with a loud clang. The people of Bletz were to be forced to witness the executions to the bitter end.

There were more shouted commands and pikemen began to push back the crowd to form two pathways — one leading from a door in the keep to a high platform on which stood an empty chair; the other from a low door near the guardhouse to the scaffold. And to add to the confusion, soldiers appeared from the guardhouse carrying flaming torches above their heads to form a ring around the mountain of wood.

In all the jostling as people were crammed tighter together, the sacking over Petr's head was suddenly dragged from his hands, leaving his face exposed. He made a grab for it, but not before the man standing next to him recognized him.

'Petr!' the peasant cried in astonishment.

'Petr?' others near by asked, turning around.

And at once, like a puff of wind, the question was being asked in all parts of the crowd.

From somewhere at the front near the scaffold, the blacksmith strained to see above the heads. 'Petr?' he shouted.

Ducking his head down, Petr signalled with a finger on his lips to the people nearest him to keep quiet. But they knew he was there and their pathetic smiles of hope and pleasure made many peasants look in their direction. Then a blast of horns brought everyone back to the grim business in hand.

Count Boleslav appeared at the doorway in the keep and the whole crowd bowed their heads as he walked to the platform, followed by the waddling figure of the priest. They were surrounded by a small escort of soldiers that included the commander of the garrison. The soldiers stood guard round the base of the platform while their commander mounted the steps and took his place beside his Lord. His practised eyes quickly scanned the crowd and the positions of the soldiers, and then settled on the scaffold. He hoped that in spite of the overnight rain it would burn quickly. He was a man of battle and had no liking for occasions such as this.

Stephan scowled in deep concentration at the richly attired figure settling into his chair. He knew he was looking at the tyrant of Bletz, but he was puzzled that the man who had life and death power over everyone should seem so unimpressive. In his imagination, Stephan had always pictured the Lord of Bletz as having giant proportions to match the enormity of his greed and cruelty, but it appeared the man was a small, trim figure of no physical power at all. His finger tugged at the knots in the twine binding the bundle and, once loosened, his hands grasped the shaft of the axe and drew it out.

Petr, who saw him do this, was startled by the sight of the weapon. Putting his hand quickly on the shaft, forcing Stephan to keep it out of sight, he whispered, 'Not yet. Not yet.'

'When?' the youth demanded. And Petr could only shake his head.

From the moment Marta had told them about Josef's fate, Petr had searched in vain for a way of rescuing his old friend. Even at this late stage his mind still turned on the problem, but with armed soldiers everywhere the task seemed more impossible than ever.

There was a general movement in the crowd as people tried to catch a glimpse of the three leaders of the uprising being pushed one by one through the low door. Their appearance was greeted with cries and sobs from relatives and friends. They were stripped to the waist and their hands were tied behind their backs. They tried to walk bravely, defiantly, but the prodding swords of the guards made them lurch and stumble.

Almost unnoticed, a fourth man — a tall, emaciated man with white hair and the remnants of clothes that were no more than filthy rags — was thrust head-first through the door. Dazzled by the light and too weak to stand, he collapsed on to the cobbles until the soldiers hauled him to his knees and dragged him to the scaffold.

Stephan knew at once that this was Josef — the man he had

come so far to see. His heart was racing, the knuckles of his hands as they gripped the axe were white, his whole body shook with rage and pity. Taking his eyes off the woodman and looking at the sky, he opened his mouth to shriek, only to find a hand firmly clamped across his lips. He flashed an angry, frustrated look at Petr who held on grimly and vehemently shook his head.

'Come now,' Petr felt the boy mouth under his hand. 'Come *now*.'

His eyes joined Stephan's on the sky and, sceptic though he was, he heard himself muttering, 'Come now. We need you — now.'

In the front ranks of the crowd, the blacksmith watched the prisoners being tied to poles projecting above the scaffold, with his mind still obsessed with the unanswered question of Petr. The thought that the man he most hated and feared might be somewhere in their midst was driving him mad. Even the voice of his partner in crime intoning a prayer for the souls of the men about to die brought no release from his torment. He looked behind him once more, scanning the rows of faces.

With only half an ear on Father Vilem, the Lord of Bletz leaned back in his chair, idly regretting that he had seen too many deaths to be excited by it any more – even, and less usually, death by burning. He watched the soldiers complete their tasks and leave the scaffold. He heard the droning voice of the priest come to an end. The rest was up to him. All that remained was for him to give the signal.

The rain had dwindled to a mere dampness in the air and he glanced at the overcast sky with the casualness of a man wondering whether it would be fine enough for a hunt. He was about to raise an arm when he heard a voice shouting, 'This is Petr speaking,' but there was no time to look down. Hurtling out of the sky with the speed and suddenness of a thunderbolt, a dark, compact body hit him squarely in the face. The blow toppled him from his chair and he fell screaming with the pain in his now sightless eyes.

Before anyone could take in what was happening — though there was a wild eagle shriek from somewhere in the crowd — the flying monster had seized the sagging flesh round the priest's mouth and ripped it open. He too collapsed on to the platform, howling and writhing in agony. But already huge wings had opened and, with deadly accuracy, the creature was attacking the soldiers holding the torches, beating men and implements of death to the ground. Without pause, the bird flew fast and low over the heads of the crowd, making peasants and soldiers alike throw themselves on the ground to escape the thrashing wings and outstretched talons.

Stephan, who was one of the very few still on his feet, was jumping up and down, waving his arms and shrieking at the top of his voice. 'Eagle! Eagle!' he screamed with tears of joy streaming down his face. And to his great delight, his guardian of old acknowledged his presence with a brief imperious screech as it wheeled round and, once more, skimmed the heads of the crowd before soaring to the tops of the walls.

One or two soldiers took wild shots at it with arrows. But, undeterred, the bird flew at them ferociously, beating them from their stations and sending them falling with agonised cries on to the crowd and cobbles below.

In the midst of this confusion, Petr gazed at the bird in speechless admiration. Its size and strength were greater than he had ever thought possible. As he watched the majestic bird leaving a trail of havoc in its wake, whatever doubts he had entertained about Stephan's life with the eagle were transformed into a deep conviction that every word of it was true. Seizing the opportunity to do something on his own account, he tried to rally the people round him. 'We must free the prisoners,' he shouted, struggling to get through the crowd. Stephan and some of the others began to follow, but they were soon blocked by the mass of people and the lines of soldiers that had formed under the barking orders of their commander.

To his horror, Petr saw smoke rising from the scaffold and, realizing that one of the torches must have fallen on to the kindling, he appealed again for help.

'This is Petr speaking,' he shouted, with hands cupped round his mouth. 'Get the men from the fire.'

But no one seemed able to move.

The scar-faced commander, who had also seen the smoke, heard the shout, but he was determined to keep the crowd back from the scaffold and the platform on which his injured master and the priest lay screaming for help. He bellowed at his soldiers to stand firm.

The blacksmith heard the shout, but he could only think of finding the owner of the voice and even now was trying to force a path through the crowd, hitting out at anyone who stood in his way.

Stephan had also heard Petr and, trying to make himself heard above the din, he began to shriek to the ever-circling eagle.

Meanwhile, the damp wood was drying fast and smoke was starting to turn to naked flames.

Just when all seemed to be lost, Stephan saw the eagle hesitate and then come flying towards him. The people round about, who had been listening open-mouthed to the frightening cries of the strange youth, fell to their knees or covered their heads in their hands. But instead of being attacked, they were amazed to see the bird hover over the boy and grip the shaft of the axe that he was holding above his head. They saw and heard the wings beating the air to create a turbulence that was like a sudden gale blowing on their faces.

For a moment, Stephan's feet left the ground, only to touch earth again as the wings failed to get their heavy burden airborne. Shrieking encouragement, he urged the bird to try again. Once more, the wings thrashed and, with every muscle in its body straining, it slowly lifted Stephan from the ground.

The sight of the boy being carried just above their heads stopped everyone in their tracks. Noise and confusion were frozen in a moment of petrified silence as the giant eagle laboured with rasping breaths to reach the scaffold. Then the silence gave way to muttered prayers and cries of fear as people thought they must be witnessing the judgement of God or an act of the Devil. Even soldiers, with weapons hanging limply at their sides, crossed themselves.

Once over the scaffold, the eagle dropped Stephan and flew off to a high perch to recover.

For the first time in his life, the commander of the garrison found himself indecisive. He could see the youth attacking the ropes binding the prisoners with wild swings of the axe. But he could not bring himself to have him stopped. Even when the leaders of the uprising threw themselves from the scaffold and one or two peasants ran forward to give support, he could not find the voice to have them seized. He felt the eyes of his soldiers on him, waiting for his orders, but the world he had known seemed to be turning on its head and he no longer knew what to do.

So no one moved. Like spectators at a play, peasants and soldiers alike were held spellbound while Stephan severed the ropes holding the woodman to the pole. They gasped as the poor man, weakened from months in prison and overcome with smoke, collapsed on to the scaffold, and anxiously watched the boy put his arms around the man and drag him from the fire.

A great shout of relief and triumph went up from the crowd. And, suddenly, they were on the move.

The commander of the garrison sprang immediately into action, shouting commands at soldiers near by to remove the injured men from the platform and get them to safety. Some fought with flailing swords to keep back the crowd, while others carried the pathetic creature who had once been the most feared man in Bletz. A third detachment, unable to lift the quivering hulk of the priest, dragged him by his legs into the great hall of the castle.

The lofty chamber did not remain a safe haven for long. Within seconds of the rescue party's arrival, the crowd broke though the cordon of soldiers outside and came flooding in like a tidal wave. Years of suffering had turned the peasants of Bletz into a baying mob whose one thought was revenge. Some carried the torches that had been intended as instruments of execution, others held smouldering timbers pulled from the fire. With wild shouts and chants they set light to the tapestries, toppled the huge table and made a fire of the chairs. They wrestled and fought like madmen with the soldiers who came running in from outside. There were deaths and injuries on both sides, but nothing could stop the dirty, calloused hands from reaching the cowering tyrant and his abject priest.

Outside the empty scaffold burned unattended, filling the courtyard with acrid smoke. People still clamoured to get into the great hall; others ran about in all directions, yelling and screaming. Small children who had been separated from their parents cried in terror. The old and sick clutched each other for support. A few people, who seemed oblivious of the mayhem going on around them, wandered about looking for relatives among the bodies lying on the cobbles. A group of young mothers, with children clinging to their skirts and infants in their arms, hurried towards the gates where some old women were already struggling to draw back the heavy bolts across the doors.

Petr sat on the cobbles with his back against a wall where he had been pushed by the movement of the crowd. The confusion in the courtyard and the sounds of the wild scenes going on inside the castle sickened and frightened him. He had always wanted to see the people of Bletz freed from the indignities of life under their tyrannical Lord, but he had never wanted it to be done like this. It should have been done lawfully. *Lawfully*. Continuity, continuity, was the word that kept pounding in his brain. But what sort of continuity could there be after a blood bath like this?

He saw the bundle he had brought with him lying forgotten on the cobbles and, for no particular reason, got up to retrieve it. He had not gone very far when he was hailed by a familiar voice bellowing his name. It was Hans, armed with a sword that had been dropped in all the confusion. Beside him, as ever, was Vislav, armed with a pike.

Petr was almost too weary in spirit to move, but some instinct for self-preservation made him run to gather up his bundle. Holding it ready to defend himself, he circled away to the open nearer the fire. His adversaries roared with laughter and pursued him with the arrogant leisure of men sure of victory.

It was their laughter that drew Stephan's attention. His elation at rescuing the prisoners had been blurred by the sudden eruption of the crowd. Surrounded by fighting peasants and soldiers, he had huddled over the semi-conscious figure of Josef in an attempt to protect him from kicking feet and heaving bodies. And when the soldiers had given way and the mob had surged past, Marta had joined them and he had stood back as she threw herself on the ground to cradle her husband in her arms. Now the noise of laughter made him look up and, seeing Petr confronted by two armed assassins, he picked up the axe which was lying near by and, shrieking, lurched into the fray.

Two against two, they dodged and thrust at each other. Then a wild swing from Stephan that sent the axe flying from his hands caught Vislav off balance. The man toppled backwards, tripping against a log jutting out from the fire and, before he could save himself, he was falling helplessly into the flames.

Petr would have tried to reach Vislav, but his way was

blocked by Hans who was bearing down on him with his sword scything the air. Stephan quickly seized the pike and shouting, 'Death to all tyrants,' he hurled himself at the blacksmith. There was just time for Hans to look round before the weapon was rammed into his chest.

Hans stood for a moment, with a look of astonishment on his face, suspended between life and death. He managed to gasp to Petr, 'Who is he?' and to hear the reply, 'The woodman's son,' before falling to the ground. The bully of Bletz died, untypically, without making another sound.

His death was celebrated by two jubilant shrieks — one from the youth proudly standing over him, the other from the bird slowly spiralling down from its high perch.

For Petr, it brought an overwhelming sense of sorrow. He knew he should be gladdened by the blacksmith's death, but he could not find it in his heart to praise the youth for what he had done. He managed to convey with a look his gratitude to Stephan for saving his life. Then, with an apologetic shrug, he walked slowly away to find his old friends, Josef and Marta.

Stephan watched him go, puzzled by his silence. Then he felt a sudden draught of air as the eagle landed beside him. With its golden head fully erect and beak tilted, it looked at him with stern approval. Then, abruptly, it uttered an inviting croak that made Stephan's face light up with joy. Ignoring everything around him — the noise, the blazing timber, the sullen faces that had edged forwards to peer at the body of the blacksmith; forgetting his parents, Petr, even the difficulty the eagle had in carrying him to the scaffold; and thinking only of those far-off days of flight, Stephan knelt down and eagerly waited for the bird to hop on to his shoulders.

The talons tightened their grip. The powerful wings began to move. In one supreme effort, the proud creature heaved itself and the boy into the air. It was desperately fighting for control with only its will to drive it on but, between gasping breaths, it managed one hoarse shriek that said, He is still mine!

Faces, full of wonder and awe, gazed out of the smoke as the miraculous pair soared above the castle walls and disappeared from sight.

'Who is the cripple?' a voice cried. And Petr, who was kneeling beside Marta and Josef, angrily shouted, 'He's the woodman's son — Stephan.'

25

O h! the joy of feeling the wind on your face, pulling at your hair. To look down and see the earth passing effortlessly beneath you. To be suspended in space with the freedom of the sky before you!

The end came just beyond the village with furrowed fields beneath them. The labouring wings faltered, struggled to resume, then ceased. There was a small screech of pain coupled with a shout of alarm, and the earth came rushing up to meet them. Bird and youth crashed together in a confusion of feathers and limbs.

Bruised and winded, but unhurt, Stephan picked himself up, and wiped the mud from his face. He looked at the eagle. It was lying very still, with its wings spread across the furrows and its proud head half buried in the ground among the small green shoots of the harvest yet to come. A light breeze played with the feathers, giving them the illusion of life.

With an agonised cry, Stephan threw himself at the bird and for a while lay with his arms around the lifeless form, sobbing as though his heart would break. When at last his tears were spent, he got to his knees and very tenderly, folded the huge wings to the body. Bearing the eagle cradled in his arms like a child, he stood up and, with his eyes on the distant mountains, slowly limped away.

Bartholomew was quietly milking the goats when he saw a distant figure approaching through the trees. At first he thought his old eyes were deceiving him. Then, with a smile that lit up his lined face, he dropped the pot of milk and, leaving the bleating goat to look after itself, ran as fast as his legs would carry him to meet the advancing youth.

The sight of the dead bird, which Stephan had carried in his arms throughout the long, arduous journey over the mountains, brought the old man to a stop. Then overcome with pity at the exhausted state of its bearer, he rushed forward with outstretched arms.

Too weary to smile or weep, Stephan greeted his old teacher with the simple statement, 'The eagle came back. . . .' They buried the once-majestic creature in the clearing — a place haunted with memories. When it was done, Bartholomew tried in vain to encourage Stephan to go with him, and he returned alone to the hut.

He put fresh logs on the fire and took the Bible from its box. But his head was too full of questions — about the past and future — to concentrate on reading and he sat with it in his hands looking towards the open door.

Hours passed and Stephan remained motionless, sitting cross-legged and staring with an almost ferocious intensity at the fresh mound of earth. His head swam with pictures that were for ever in movement and often blurring into one another — mountain peaks and crags, tree tops and huge vistas of the open sky. In his ears was an endless cacophony of sounds — rippling air, howling winds and, above them all, the raucous imperative cries of a bird.

As the sun went down, a cold wind began to blow, wafting the smoke from Bartholomew's fire in his direction. For the first time he stirred, tossing his hair in a gesture learned from his old guardian. Head proudly erect, eyes on the darkening sky, he uttered one long and mighty shriek in praise of the great golden eagle.

Postscript

The commander of the garrison had never been one for arguments — whether receiving orders or giving them — and he was in no mood for arguments now. For many days he had had soldiers patrolling the village and clearing the debris left by the riot. With the keep little more than a charred shell, he had given orders that as soon as the deputation of peasants arrived they were to be brought to the guardhouse. Nervously, they waited to hear what he had to say.

'I do not propose,' he began, 'to discuss the matter of —' he gave a helpless gesture with a gloved hand '— that bird and the youth. I understand the cripple is the same one who was once judged to be the Devil's creature. That is in the past. What *we* saw is . . . ,' the stern voice hesitated, '. . . is difficult to explain. But it happened and that is as much as any of us can say. I don't propose to discuss it.' He cleared his throat, drew himself up and addressed the peasants with the utmost severity.

'What the people of Bletz have done would, under normal circumstances, bring a sentence of death to every man in the village — and it may yet do so. But I know the hardships you've suffered and the punishments you've received, many of them on my orders. My duty has always been to carry out the commands of the Lord of Bletz. Now, the Lord is dead, and so is the priest. So, too, are some of my men, and many of your kin also. Not one of them has had a Christian burial and we must pray their spirits don't haunt this place.

'I do not find it fitting for me to rule, though I could do so with loyal men around me. But something must be done — and done quickly. Make no mistake, this crime will not remain a secret for long. As the wind carries the seeds, the news will soon reach the ears of people beyond Bletz. And what then? More reprisals? More deaths?

162

'To prevent this, I've decided to send letters to our late Lord's sister, married to Prince Broucek. These will state that the deaths and damages were caused by an accidental fire. They'll also request she asks her Lord to take possession of all the lands, property and peasants belonging to Count Boleslav. I shall give strict orders to my men to keep the real cause of the fire to themselves, and I advise you to tell your kinsmen to do the same. Do you agree?'

'We agree,' the peasants said with one voice.

'Miller!' the commander continued without pause, looking sternly at Petr. 'You know as well as I do that you return to Bletz with a sentence of death hanging over you. I've thought carefully about this and have decided to be merciful. I take it on myself to rescind the sentence of banishment and, instead, order you to be headman once more.'

'I'm an old man —,' Petr started to protest.

'I say you will be headman,' the soldier impatiently barked. 'Do you understand?'

And, having no alternative, Petr gravely nodded.

'Now go. And see that everything's as it should be when your new Lord or his deputy arrives.'

The peasants meekly bowed and began to file out.

'Continuity,' Petr thought. 'We may yet achieve continuity.'

But was that enough? Was it enough to see their lives return to the way they were? Were they to forget what had happened and accept that the deaths were simply to replace the old tyrant with a new one? Surely they should strive for something more than that?

He paused for a moment at the door and turned back to the august military figure.

'What sort of man is Prince Broucek?' he dared to ask.

'He's a great lord,' was the summary reply.

'But is he fair?'

'Fair? D'you mean the colour of his hair?'

163

'I mean, is he just?'

'*Just?*' The soldier gave a rueful chuckle that allowed Petr a glimpse of the man behind the imposing uniform. 'We'll just have to wait and see.'

Petr nodded and stepped out into the cool sunshine in the courtyard. The blackened walls of the keep opposite made him suddenly wish that it could be left like that — as a reminder. Then instinctively his eyes turned to the sky. The clouds were high and moving swiftly across the patches of blue. On top of this, his mind superimposed another image, clearer than the sky itself and one that he knew would stay with him for the rest of his life — a boy and an eagle flying together.

'Was it a miracle?' he asked himself.

He shook his head and hurried away, relishing the freedom to be among friends and ready to join whatever struggles they might have to face in the future.

The Hill of the Red Fox

Allan Campbell McLean

'Unknown man found shot' said the newspaper headline. Alasdair recognised the man he had met on the train to Skye, the man who had slipped him a desperate last message 'Hunt at the Hill of the Red Fox M15'.

Alasdair finds the Hill of the Red Fox on Skye, but the note still makes no sense. Nor at first do most of the strange and dangerous goings on on the island, many of which involve Alasdair's sinister uncle, Murdo Beaton. There is much more than the odd bit of poaching happening— atomic scientists and their secrets are disappearing.

People are not always what they seem. Whom can Alasdair really trust? In finding out he uncovers a web of espionage—and all its perils!

ISBN 0 86241 055 X   (age 10+)   £1.95

Escape from Loch Leven

Mollie Hunter

When Mary, Queen of Scots, arrives at Loch Leven Castle, a reluctant 'guest' at the mercy of her treacherous lords, it is not long before her legendary beauty and charm win the hearts of her captors and the passionate devotion of young Will Douglas, the orphan page boy.

Yet for all the elaborate schemes of her loyal band of followers, it is the ingenuity and courage of the young page which secure her release and the chance to regain her crown.

There can be few who do not know the final fate of the tragic young queen, yet Mollie Hunter has succeeded in recapturing the atmosphere of intrigue, excitement and hope which surrounded her in captivity.

ISBN 0 86241 137 8   (age 11+)   **£1.95**

Haki the Shetland Pony

Kathleen Fidler

There is no future for Adam Cromarty on his
parents' croft in the Shetlands. Should he sell his
beloved pony Haki, whom he has cared for and
trained since birth, to buy a ticket for the
mainland where there is more chance of a job?
Adam cannot bring himself to do this so he
makes a deal with a circus owner that he can only
buy Haki if he takes him too as trainer.

They settle well into the different but exciting
life of the circus and Haki is a great success with
the audience. But Adam makes a bitter enemy:
Willy Baxter, in charge of the chimps, is jealous
of Adam's success. He tries to injure Haki and
eventually succeeds, although the circus elephant,
with whom Haki has an extraordinary
relationship, steps in to prevent total disaster.

"This is a gripping and sometimes heart-rending
tale. The plot and characterisation of both people
and animals are first rate— Kathleen Fidler has
excelled herself again."

ISBN 0 86241 075 4 (age 8 +)   £1.75